Uber

John Robinson

Contents

1 : Preface

Note from the author

Without perhaps knowing the exact meaning of the word, I did think that 'Uber' meant 'beyond', or 'the elite'. However, a close friend of mine Michael, who can also speak more than one language, told me that it means 'above'. Which is also fine.

Probably the key thing I want you the reader to understand is that this word, although somewhat hijacked by the personal car for hire/taxi company's usage (not to mention Macdonald's food delivery service), has a aetiology which goes much further and deeper, than this use of the name.

So why have I chosen this as the title? Well I'd say, on top of the conflict with language, which is a pretty much consistent idea across my writing, is that I like to think that there is more to life than my hospital admissions, my various crimes and other misdemeanours, and other spelling/grammatical errors, such as my life has presented itself with.

We go through our lives like as journeys. Sometimes slow, sometimes fast like in a blink of an eye. And remembering them back can be lucid, or painful. Yet we try. We try with our families, with our education and various pastimes.

And work if we can hold down a
job.

Society is a collective effort. A
communal monument, that has
taken Milena to attain. And the
recent break down in civilized
behaviour across America,
triggered by the slaughter of one
black man Lloyd George, and
consequent crack down by the
state, if anything demonstrates
how much further we must go.

Yet, despite perhaps not
talking about this in my university
essays, even though maybe I
should have been, in this world we
sign a contract, from the day we
breach the womb, screaming and
kicking, until we lay down on our
final resting place at the end. A
contract with our neighbours,

families, and communities that we will work towards the greater good. And if we break this agreement? Well then there will be consequences.

This book steals from a photograph, a moment, a single memory, or the time I was in police custody. Faced with questions from the powers above, and how they were able to squeeze the facts out of me. Despite only displaying a single moment, I have in fact been arrested and indeed held, on numerous occasions to date, and I can draw from all of these, in revealing this experience henceforth.

Without giving anything more away, see how you like it?

John

2 : At your mercy

One sunny Sunday morning JoJo was woken up early by the phone. "JoJo, we have a problem. We need you to attend the surgery, at Nine hundred hours".Oh God, I thought, what is this about, what have I done?

So, nearing the time, I pulled on some clothes, washed my face, brushed the teeth, and took foot out of my house.

I gingerly maneuverer over to the bus stop and hesitated before climbing into the steel beast. Finally arriving in town, I called dad :

"Dad, It's Joey. Can you give me a lift to the doctor's?"

"Hi Joseph, not today, I am busy, what's the matter? I haven't heard you like this way for a while?"
"Oh god dad, really?"
"Really!"

So just as it was beginning to rain drizzle, I buttoned up my coat, and began to make the half hour journey to the doctor's surgery.

When I got there, and after a brief ten minutes wait, the doctor came out of his office, and gestured me into his study. Sitting there, Jack my nurse, Pierre my dad, and a couple of thirty something unknown females…

"What's this all about?" I stammered, struggling to catch my breath.

"We have a problem JoJo… Or more precisely a number of them…"

"Go on?" I pleaded.

"Well for starters, what is this I hear about you getting in to fights, on the street?"

I investigated his irises for sympathy, but found none…

"You mean the fight I had with Will a few weeks ago outside my house. The one where I ripped his jacket?"

"I wasn't aware of that one, but go on?"

"Hold on Doctor B., that wasn't even a fight, we were sparring, like randori. Me and Will have both had some martial arts training, so we were just practicing our skills?"

"And you ripped his jacket? That's personal property you do know?"
"Hold on. He thumped me in my head. If I had let him continue, I could have ended seriously injured… I closed the distance, and attempted to drop him to the floor… I didn't hurt him though.

I'm sure that jacket of his, I ripped, well he'd nicked it from me anyway a while ago before…"
"You call him your friend, and this is the same guy who nicked your jacket? What kind of a friend is that?"

"Sure, Doctor Will is a mate", I struggled to explain. "He's a mate, so I don't mind if he nicks my stuff and reports me to the authorities. Look he even took a video of the fight, you can see for yourself that there was no aggression, no ill will…" I handed the doctor my phone, with the video, and he put it to one side.

Then my dad spoke… "Or what about that time you beat him up in town, in Derby city centre. That was reported to us, by the city wardens you know?"

I said, "but dad, whose side are you on anyway. I play you chess most days in the coffee shops of Derby, let you win most of the time. Okay perhaps that's taking some artistic license, I try to beat you. And I'd say at least three quarters of the time, fail. So why are you ganging up against me when I need this help most of all?"

"Settle down JoJo" my dad replied.

"No one is here to get you. We are all here for your best interests, that's all".

"Okay" the good doctor continued. "Please tell us more about what happened in the city centre, with your friend Will?"

"Okay doctor" I went on. "This one wasn't videoed, and it appears that someone witnessed it, and maybe reported us."
"Sure, go on?"
"Yes, so I had been watching some Gracie Jujitsu videos, which I purchased a while ago direct from America. And don't even ask what the duties where I had to pay for the postage.

Well anyway, a good deal of Gracie Jujitsu is groundwork. So, me and Will got down on the grass, and tried out some of these moves. Grappling, escaping, trapping, closing the distance (to avoid strikes), and such with."

"And you think this is an okay pastime, to be carrying out in the city centre, at midday? Is it hardly any surprise that a member of the public, or caretaker, reported you?"

"Again doctor, it was by two consenting adults. I really don't see what the big fuss is about?"

"Okay" doctor B seemed pushed for time now. "I think we have heard enough. Let me introduce me to my two colleagues here… B here is a student nurse, and K is a social worker. If you can give us a few moments alone to discuss your case, then we will feed back our findings. P if you will stay with us, okay?"

I wanted to say, Dad, stop it, can't you see what they are doing? Why can't you be on my side, for once in your life…

But these words fell on deaf ears.

I was led back into the waiting area, and what started as a few minutes, turned in to the best part of an hour, before they finally called me back in to eternal furnace of a decision which remains with me to this day.

"Joey we have decided to section you on section One : One : Seven of the mental health acts. We have deemed you to be a risk to yourself and others. Which is largely owing to your noncompliance with your prescription medication. But also, the things you have done and said, both on and off this drug. Getting in to fights with strangers on the streets, as well as talking about inappropriate positions with street girls, is both offensive as much as it is potentially dangerous. And this is to say nothing of the offensive language you have peppered your books with over the years, betrayals of confidence including name dropping, and a host of other unsatisfactory decisions, have left us with no choice. We are depriving you of your liberty and can only pray that you do learn to behave yourself, and that is if you ever want to get out!

You are henceforth admitted to a local psychiatric locked ward."
At that point two healthy well pressed and smelling of aftershave policemen entered the room.
"Please don't struggle JoJo, you can't singlehandedly take on the system and expect to win!"

3 : From Baby Steps to Victory

Let's look at martial arts now. There is a hidden code, bequeathed to those with skills in the martial arena, which entitles them, and no one else, to defend humanity against the scourge of the Earth. This is the martial way, the way of the kantana, Budo.

But there is a saying 'play with fire, and you will get burned'. And indeed, when he burnt that first bridge, JoJo feared that he was exiled forever. In a flash something had happened. Something had changed inside him. A piece of his soul had been lost. That spark in his eyes, doused. And from that day forth, every day, he had to make amends. To attempt to heal the rift in cosmic Karma, that only he had instigated. To heal the damage caused by his crimes. And only he could do it. No one else. To amend the sins of himself, and his fathers, and their fathers before them. His father's father's forefathers! To take time out and pray. To heal the wounds of four generations. Across the seas and the mountains. To do what had never been done. To bring peace, to the world.

Then it falls on every sentient being, to heal and recover, and build and imagine.

The martial way begins with baby steps. The first breath, taken from the first people. And every new-born babe, remembers this beginning. So on-wards to victory!

The tournament was announced, and quickly built momentum. By the traditional channels, and the more erst ones of word of mouth, bird and carrier pigeon.

Before long people from all over the world, were applying, and testing their mettle by this the trial of fire. Some contenders with natural ability, strength, speed or discipline. Others returning, failing, flailing, and yet trying again. And again, and again. Until yet beaten and trod upon, they sank deep into the recess of the wombs of the Earth. Lest they sourced new strength, and rose high once more, like the eternal Phoenix, lifts her wings above the tomb of her death.

Indeed, as Christ our Saviour, returned from his death. Some lost, other's won. It's all part of the game. For domination, survival. And ultimate glory.

The contest was relentless. People died. Every day. Good souls returning to the heaven from whence they came. Ashes to ashes, dust to dust. And the papers? How did the popular media account for these unprecedented fatalities?

With grim, macabre morose, to be sure. Sometimes the truth was told. But so often, between the axe of the butcher's clavicle sever-age to the cold stone slab of the coroner's mortuary, sometimes the truth, gets replaced with their truth. And the truth? Lost somewhere between the volumes of the medical students, and their superiors the consultants, and the police.

So even when the coroners could find no distinct discernible cause, JoJo had his suspicions. And he vowed not to go out like a lab rat. When they gassed his room, and gasping he had to crawl to the floor. Begging for breath, and for life. Not when they sent him up to chimney, or locked him away in seclusion, for shift after shift after shift. He had come this far. And he sure wasn't going to let the grim reaper stop him now. Not today. Not today.

Death the final way. We are born. We live. We die. Three absolute truths. If we are lucky, we have the chance to make some a positive impact, in-between these absolutes. Sometimes, but not always. We try our best.
Kung Fu is about more than just the feet. It's about more than just the palms. It is a way of living, a way of life. A commitment to positive breath, positive diet, positive exercise. And if you fall foul to many of the ailments that this postmodern world affronts us with? Take respite and take solace. No one ever said it would be easy. But for these challenges that beset

us, there will be calm after the storm. Hopefully you will get better. Every day, easier after the trauma. Healing takes time. It can take years. Sometimes a lifetime.

Whilst it is true that I have yet to recreate the successes still fully I have had on the written page, with my own personal martial career. I've got my yellow belt. It took a certain amount of rigor to attain this rank, and I'm not sure that I'll ever have the nerve to step back on those dojo mats. But even if not, I've got what they gave me. And there are some moves that, when learned, you never forget. And I have been adding to my repertoire. From kicks, to take downs, to strikes. Like I said before, there is a lot to be learned. Another lifelong progress if we are lucky anyway. Do not fear your enemies, make them fear you. And only you can do this.

4 : The Ultimate Crime

The official secrets act is a tricky one. It requires you not to discuss your business.
You can't talk about the people you have killed, the missions you have been on. The prostitutes you have eaten, or the payments you earned, beyond the remit of the mission. Which means at all.

Not to your family or friends. Not to anyone.

Remember that spy from a few years back, who was found

bound and gagged, inside a small suitcase in his flat. And the suitcase was zipped up.

Cause of death? Asphyxiation, suicide. Even though it is physically impossible to tie yourself up, and close the case, in this way. And it's not just me saying that. A private investigator was hired and came to this same conclusion.

It was obvious that this spy, working for the MI6/MI5 UK secret services, had outstepped his bounds... Perhaps he had breached the terms of his contract or done something deemed to be inexcusable. Or at least upset some of this colleague? I can't say. Without further inside knowledge, I'm not able to discern any further detail, with regards to his death.

Just that it seems highly unlikely, if
possible, for this man to have
killed himself, in this way. But
without further information we
will never know.

....

Or how about a few years ago
when the 'Phillpotts' a man with
three wives and like ten children,
burnt down the government flat
they were living in, killing most of
their kids, and now locked away
for good?

I have difficulty
understanding how this is possible
for a man to do this, having a
family myself. I can't see it.

Please understand that the
fire was started at the front door
letter box. Like somebody poured

petrol through it, set it on fire, and watched the house burn.

The official verdict was that the couple did it, to claim on the insurance. But If that was so, then why didn't they rescue the kids, and escape, before destroying the property?

I don't need to see psychological evaluations of the pair, to determine their unfitness to be parents.

They were both crying in court. And what did you expect? These two have gone from full and rich lives, to lonely inside of cells, for the indefinite future, and will never see their kids again. Who could ask this for anyone, even their worst enemies?

I understand that the couple did have a lot of enemies gaging from the public sentiment, the reaction in the press, and on the internet. Please just give me a minute. All it would have taken was for one, or possibly a couple of these haters, to pour the petrol through the door, and walk away.

No one would ever know any the better. And it gives definite closure to the problem of the Phillpott's.

I know I could be wrong, that this opinion I have just stated, is just that. It is neither ratified, nor evidenced, by anything other than my common sense, and deeply felt intuition. People are capable of the most terrible things, and the murder of these children, be it by an unknown assassin, or the parents, is surely such a crime.

Without further evidence, this is yet another conspiracy.

What else, the death of princess Diana? The USA's first space landings? The whole rotten mess which was the (second) invasion of Iraq?

There are more questions than there are answers, and it is easy to come to an early determination, without inside evidence or information.

Each of us must make our ways through this life, finding our own answers to these questions that life throws at us. Some of us will make it, some will be tested, others will fall. And yet there will be people who will rise above our enemies, war away from the fires or pain, and venture on to the much-forsaken golden Nirvana. The fire which consumes and destroys, Is the same fire that binds and forges the sharpest of blades. The very blades that decapitate the heads of tyrants of third world dictators, and innocents alike. That cut the cords of the mothers of new-born babes and complete the genesis of new life.

We need the lovers, as we need the mothers. We need good people, to hold each other in communion and recognition, of each other's accomplishments onwards.

This book has taken me the best part of a year to write. It covers new territory, as well as new looks at the old. I find writing therapeutic, gives me a chance to break free from the shackles of the lived world, and be born again in the literary one. I was considering attempting to get a publisher, or an agent at least. But given that the two I have sent precursors to, have both neglected to respond, I am now looking again at the concept of self-publishing. Once I have finished this third draft, then I can look at getting the cover finished (as designed by a dear family member), and even create a Kindle Direct Publishing advert blurb, to promote this work on Kindle.

I think the final edition of this book will be good to read, and hopefully good enough to buy. I am not looking at setting high sales cost. Hell, I may even set the royalties to zero, to promote maximum sales potential. But it would be nice to make some small cash from this release. I'll drink to that.

5 : The Contract

"Slow down. You've committed crimes. I know that, you know that, you don't need to repeat them."

"So?"

"So, that is a serious offense. But like I already said, we don't need to go there. That is old territory, I'm here to ask you something else?"

"What? Can you at least loosen up these cuffs on my wrists?"

A nod, and another figure steps from the darkness, and it is done.

"So, if you are not bothered about mass genocide, then why the hell are you keeping me here?"

"Because…" the power stated… "I have a proposition to make you…"

"I want you to listen to me carefully, and only answer when you have given it sufficient thought, maybe sleep on it…"

"You've pricked my ears, go on…"

"So, this is that… We want you to work for us. Complete the missions we send you, and become an employee of your crown?"

"And if I refuse?"

"Well then of course, you can return… Return to your pathetic excuse of a life. Day to day, no glory, no honour, no payback…."

"And if I agree?"

"Well then you will become one of us, hidden. But know this : we will

take no recognition if you get
caught. If you get caught, you will
have to pay for your crimes, and
this default, this excursion, this
exemption, will hold no ground in
a court of law... there can be no
mercy for your type. If you are
caught again you will have to pay.
Those few years you've already
served will feel like a walk in the
park compared to your next
sentence. Do you hear me. We're
not messing about!"

"You're not messing about. I get
that... So, what's in it for me?"

"Sex. A given... Money... Okay
sure... A house, a nice flat in a nice
neighbourhood, with nice friendly
neighbours, a laptop, a state-of-the-
art digital gaming platform, with
connection, and games, yes you get

all that… What more do you want?"

"Anonymity. A shelter from my enemies. I have already escaped more than two assassination attempts. I'm not sure how much longer I can maintain this side…"

"Done. I don't think you quite understand how this works. We are the powers that be, we are your friends. And if you trash us, we will catch you, and become your worst nightmare. So how does all of that sound?"

A beat, (a pause) and then…

"Where do I sign?"

6 : Life's Problems

So, let me ask you a question…
What should I do?

My life seems to have plateaued,
and as I stand on the edge of the
precipice, I think I can hear my
bells a calling.

I am torn. Do I move with
my heart or my head? Do I do the
right thing? And the right thing by
God?

We have striven so hard for
all these years.

My beacon, my pride, my
joy.
It's hard you know. To say
goodbye to our dreams. To act
with nonchalance, as if everything
is okay.

Was the doubting JoJo had been
right all the time? To let the lies,
the doubts, the fears become true.
That the past counts for nothing,

that this uncertainty is only the future we have?

You say I should cease and depart? To pretend that she means nothing to me. That this union is a waste of time? For me to listen to all the haters, the naysayers, and discard this palace, which we have built over the last nineteen years? Even when I threw away the hope a long, long time ago.

How do I pretend that I don't have pride? That I don't have a heart. That the wounds of the past, and damage already done are years that we won't be able to get back.

Wait, there is a problem. This is the woman I have shed tears for. What about her? The light of our lives, keeps us both going…

Who when her daughter was troubled with a serious flu, struggling, I sat by her bedside soothing the pain until she was better?

Tell me to shut up.
Tell me to move on.
They say children are the most important thing. That a marriage is nothing, a piece of paper.

But what is love? Something shared? The onus of a singularity, or the crux of a duo? Until death we do part.

I need to write my will. I think today marks my halfway point. In fact, it is only a matter of days until my Thirty Eighth birthday. This was the year the age, my once best friend scruffy Nick didn't reach. I need to do it for Nick. As he looks down in heaven over me, over us.

I attended his funeral, and he is sleeping now. We all meet our maker one day.

I need to do the right thing. I need to place my daughter, and my wife above me…

I'm not going to let them go. I need to stay strong, not just for me or my love, but also for her child. We have eternity ahead of us. To let go of the past. Yet still hold on to those few happy memories that remain.

Who said it was easy? It marks the end of an era. The end of one act of the play and transition in to a new one.

When I married her, and for all these years I have spent in hospital, I have kept a seat in my heart next to her.

Being the end of an era, is okay. With closure comes the beginning of a new one. As my medication takes effect, and my breathing gets stronger, I can make new friends. And we as a family, can create new memories. Moments of truth, forged in the fires of pain and capture, and released and realized in the bliss which is calm and strength.

One day we will all leave this Earth, and return to our fathers and forefathers, and mothers and other ancestors. We must make the most of the hands presented to us. The people we meet, and the relationships we can nurture.

I once got caught in a honey trap. I decided to go to the police station and put it on record my side of the story, so if this ever came to light, I had already made my recollection of the event. That was executed by an unknown entity who told me he had already forced convictions of several high-profile personalities, in this manner. I was lucky it wasn't me.

I even heard some years later that an individual who had been setting up these social media honey-traps, had himself been snared. I am confident that this idiot got his come up-pence. After these terrible events, I ran to people who bled me for all I was worth. Stripping me both of my health, my wealth, and very nearly my marriage. Thank god those moments are over!

Where do we go from here?
I need to build one my strengths. My writing sure, but also my reading. To continue to pay off my bills and credit cards, until I don't owe anything. To continue to support my better half, as she continues to visit me. And maintain good relationships with my other family members, and friends as best I can. That should be enough.

7 : Who I am fighting?

"So where are we going now JoJo? What is your plan, your goal, your ending?

Who is your enemy?"

"I once considered Shadow to be my enemy…"

"Who is he?"

"Some black guy. No not that, not him…"

"Why not?"

"Well I met a few black African English men, on the wards. And they were cool. Nice guys normally. Hell, I even went over to East Africa, and spent some weeks on a locked ward there. And the crew were quite exceptional to me. Hell, I felt like a king. They treated me well, well. I value that…"

"So, if not 'shadow' then who else?"

"Well the National Health Service, despite trying their best, have kept me behind locked wards for far too many years, I mean over four,

where I was in 'servitude' to their
care. Sure, they may have been
trying their best, but how can I
forget these years stolen from me? I
cannot forget, much less forgive
them for taking away some of the
best years of life. Sure, the world
carries on revolving like it always
has done, but mine was trapped."
"Without naming names, all of
these consultants, and judges, and
men and women, who saw my
torment within these seconds,
minutes, hours, days, weeks,
months and finally years, to the
same buildings, the same beds, the
same dining rooms. Where was the
sense in that? The mercy, the
healing? Where was the
protection? The logic, the reason?"
"I can't forget this, much less
forgive."

"The best I can do is try and move on. Make a success with the rest of my life, for what years I have left. To try and build a sandcastle, which has repeatedly been knocked down by the playground bullies, again and again. To beat them, by making something of my life, whereas they have only ever written me off. This has taken some doing!"

8 : University

"So, what are you going to do now?"
"How can you make progress, much less heal, where there is always this pressure to perform?"
"You can please note that in the final three years of my five year

degree, where I took on Theatre Studies, as a part of my joint honours Bachelor of Arts undergraduate university degree, at no point was I allowed on stage. In fact, I was even told categorically that *all* part time students, were *not* allowed to act. Even through a couple of years later I met another joint honour student theatre student, who told me she had done just that : acted in the year's annual production."

"Which just goes to show… It is one rule for some, and another for everyone else! I had originally hoped that my theatre excursion would get me some live dramatic performances. Which I know would have been difficult, seeing as my memory is like a sieve, so I would have struggled with remembering the lines. Not to mention my breathing would have been difficult to cope with, if not for me, then the other cast and audience certainly."

"If I have learned one thing from my university career, it is that pretty everything they tell you is subject to caveats, exclusions and ad hoc conditions."

"Please don't get me wrong. It does matter, the amount of work you put it. It matters that you read the books, the online journals, and to get on well with your peers."

"Don't expect the lecturers to do your work for you."

"Hell, I was even told twice by my supervisor to proofread my dissertation draft."

"Okay I did manage to scrape a grade of 68% for my final

dissertation. Which is a strong two : one, and it was on the back of this that I was able to graduate with an upper second. But I was secretly hoping for a first for this paper. By some miracle. I was to get it, put in a lot of work, reading, research and originality, looking at mental health/schizophrenia from a lay perspective."

"With insight, with *the* insight, which is gained from year's spent on the locked wards. That the position of expert by experience gives me. An understanding the need for taking medication, as well as the aim and hope, of coming off them one day. An attempt to unravel the position of housing/social aspects/family/loved ones/and exercise aspects, into what makes

an individual become who he or she, is ultimately destined to be."
"So no, I don't buy it. Of course, I don't. How can I? But in the dissertation, I was forced to remain academic. Which meant not just espousing my deep hate of the whole psychiatric apparatus, at least not saying it explicitly."

"Rather then it became an unspoken truth. A maintenance, position. a hand, range, a defence."
"Hell, my whole degree was a position. A joint effort, between doing the readings, attending the classes, writing and presentations, to a cue, to a tea, a par, an ace. Which I didn't manage, for my modules. Hell, I think my mode average across the five years, was a third (40%). But there was such a range in the grades achieved, from

a low third to a top first, that the median average was a two : one. Or for another word, a *good* degree!

"I graduated which is proof that hard work does pay off. And if I didn't get on with the lecturers, then I was resigned to accepting the third grades they gave me. Gave me inevitably."

"So, what can we learn from this process?"
"I'd say hard work does pay off. Don't expect a degree to be handed to you on a plate. Certainly not at Derby University. And you need to try to be original. Don't take it as proof the facts you are told. Be prepared to question the truths you are handed, and those you already hold. You can carve your own path in this field. Conduct your own research, and deliberate

and craft your own insights, into whatever field you have chosen to read.

It's much like language, or *hegemony* as Gramsci once developed. The agency that individual actors, from politicians to influential academics, can impact the field, and flows and currents within. We all hope to be remembered when we die. And not for the wrong things. And even if we are all eventually forgotten, by making positive influences and impressions while we are alive, at least means that we *have* made a difference, for the good of the world.

"Read. This is important. Share your knowledge and discoveries with those around you. In an academic sense, your peers,

and more importantly your superiors the academic lecturers."
"Don't worry if the way you write, does not conform to all established norms and protocol that you are fed, elsewhere at your university career."
"We each have our own style. By attending your lectures, and reading most of the texts set, and at least some of your secondary readings as well, you earn the right to speak, think and write, in your own voice. This is your privilege. Everyone has their own style.

And the academic habitus (world), is an eternally evolving and adapting world sphere. With norms that are constantly adapting to the latest generations of students and academic papers, and new excellences across the board. These are the pinnacles you need to aim for!"

"So, did you deserve your grade?"

"Well you know, I tried my best."

"I worked hard. Even if compared to my generally younger peers, my work may not have been that impressive."

"But I did as much reading as was physically possible, spending many hours in the library, and not just playing Facebook poker (although I did this as well). I even managed to grade for my yellow belt, at a local martial arts club, in my second year. Although I had to give this up, when I found my martial studies were taking too much out of me and decided that in order to complete this education, I was going to need to give it my one hundred percent."

"A dedication which eventually gave me a voice, written, and an ear. An ability to seek out and find the truth from studies, with revelation, and compare and complete."

"So, what else should we be aware of? What should new, and returning university students know, what advice can I give you to support your own role, and position, in this eternal struggle for pole position?"

"As I have already said, you need to do the work. Attend your classes, and don't just think that because there is nobody there to penalize you for missing classes, that your attendance won't reflect in you grade. Because it will."

"Something I haven't mentioned prior, is that your

relationships with the academics. I have already said you need to build bridges with your peer group. And they are going through pretty much what you are traversing too. So, if you ever miss a class or two dues to ill health (or a hangover), they will be the ones to turn to, for lesson notes."

"It is how well you get on with those that are grading your work, will be what makes the difference between a good grade, a great grade, a pass and a fail. If they don't like you, then it is going to make it that much more difficult for you to achieve a top grade when the marks are issued."

"And no, there is not room for recourse."

"Are you sure?"

"Okay, let me give you a final example on this issue, before drawing this discussion to a close."

"Go on…"

"In our final year L a young white, European student was headed for a good first, except her final theatre play-script, was failed by a (new) lecturer, who seemed hell bent on making her own stamp on the class of 2016, by marking the student down."

"She was forced to completely redo and submit her dissertation/play, several thousand words, in a completely different style. Which was now capped at a pass (a low third). Consequently, bringing her final grade down to a lower second, and thus, as she related, stamping out her dream of gaining a masters, either here or at any other university across the country."

"So why do I think she was awarded this low grade?"
"I think because she had chosen the 'Theatre of the absurd', as her plays genre, which aims to test the audience's preconceptions of drama, with extreme and sometimes outright absurd convention breaking ideas… And the unit leader, didn't appreciate this…"

"Just as I submitted an essay to this tutor and was failed. Which basically meant I had to put in an overcharged second essay, to bring the grade up (it was averaged across the two units), to scrape a third overall."

"Was this being fair?"

"No. But I think I understand how it works? Basically, what it amounts to is this… You are the student. You are there to learn. You do what you are told. The lecturer is above you. Hell, they like it if you bow down to them like gods! They expressly don't want you to come up with *original* ideas for your undergraduate degree. Even if you thought that was the goal you were aiming for."

"As the fee payer, you need to satisfy their requirements."
"They are the ones who will be grading your work. And each essay, is double marked, so you need to pay attention, to what you are told in class. And give them back both the same ideas (content) and styles you have learned (form)."

"And remember, you are going to university to learn. To develop and improve. If your sole purpose is to spend the three years of your attendance going out drinking, clubbing, and having fun, then you will fail your degree (to say nothing of the hangovers student nights out are renown for!)"

"Equally, if you expect university to be an appendix of A levels at sixth form, where the standard of your work is as uniform, only second to the dress code of your school, you are similarly going to struggle."

"University, in effect, gives you infinitely more free time, than A levels ever did. But it is expected that you use if not all, then at least half of this time, for self-motivated study. So that means yes, going to the library and reading books, yes going on the journals, and extra internet research (which will become ever more important as you journey ever closer to your final year.)"

"And as for medical students? Well God help you. There is that much more pressure to perform, at a consistent high level, across your studies for this discipline. I was lucky to get into university in the first place, much less a STEM degree. But the fact that I did get in if anything drove me to attend and work hard come what may. I once even heard that one of my lecturers accused me of cheating across my units... She said I hacked into other students' computers, maybe if they had been left open, and stole documents. Which is the biggest load of bull I've ever heard. I didn't once cheat at my degree, not then, not before. It's something I have never done, and never plan to do. It's like telling lies, I simply don't do it. Suffice to say, that was another one of my lecturers, who gave me no grades better than a low third. Silly idiot!"

"I'm not saying *don't* enjoy yourself. Sure, go out the weekends if you want. But equally, give yourself some leeway in your approach to writing the work. And reading. Read around. Make time to explore the reading and explore your own writing styles. And when the papers submission dates loom, give yourself a good few week, a month even, to stop drinking, and get down to the *hard graft* which is for first few drafts."

"Finally remember university is only the first step in your graduate life, which will hopefully take you beyond the realms of your previous meagre existence, and jettison your way above the stratosphere, where other mere humans reside. You are going to be a graduate! You are going to have letters after your name? Well done!"

9 : Graduation

"Okay JoJo, so what can you tell me today?"
How about we talk a little bit about getting a degree?

"Okay go on, so what can you tell me about this then?"

Okay one step at a time… Firstly you know that I got my degree? And I'll go to hell if it wasn't a challenge. But both of my parents have one, as does my sister, and so you might say it runs in the family…

So, what tips can I give you? Firstly, work hard across your years at university. At first it may seem like years of luxury, seeing as most of the student time is given to reading. And how many young undergraduates do this? But don't be fooled. Take this free time as an excuse to slack off at your peril. Because if you do, when the final essays are being written, and exams taken, and you are struggling with some of the concepts being asked of, you will only have yourself to blame.

Hopefully you can use this time given, to read, in the library and at home.

Oh yes and here's another useful piece of advice, don't be afraid to buy the books on your reading list.
Whilst it isn't expected for you to read every single book on the reading list, cover to cover, you are expected to have had a good read, of at least one of two of them per unit. You also need to become familiar with the student resources (ergo journals) available to you. This is my impression anyway. Please understand that I am only one individual who conquered the system. At least managed to

graduate. But I hope that some of the pointers that I picked up along the way, can be of benefit to others who are in the process of doing so. Most of all, don't give up! The number of students who I have seen start the degree, and *not* finish, is quite alarming. But hopefully with my careful guidance, and your hard work, you will be able to avoid becoming one of these statistics!

There is a great amount of literature and knowledge out there. Make the most of it. Something I tried to do is to read at least a chapter (thirty pages or so) every day.

Don't cut corners. By the time you reach your third year, you should become a competent enough reader/writer, to be able to slow read when needed, and fast read, for the rest of the time. This is a skill that comes with time. And please pay attention to your text. Learn how to take notes, and then take notes during your lectures. Write these up on the same day when you get home.

Like I said, most of the undergraduate time is given to self-motivated study. I'm not saying you shouldn't let your hair down, every once and a while (the odd weekend for example). But for me, the truth is that the only time I went out clubbing, was after I had completed the damn thing. This was due to a combination of the fact that I was so preoccupied with the reading, and simply didn't have time. I also didn't have the friends to go out with. Then when the opportunity presented itself, I did finally let my hair down, get drunk and spend far too much money on getting other people pissed too. But that, you can say, is another story.

Student life should be some of the best years of your life. You will meet a great number of young, and eager to learn minds. And, a great wealth of expert knowledge, presented to you by your lecturers.

A trick I learned whilst on my studies, is that every lecturer, will have his or her own separate expectations of you, as to what is required to achieve a passing grade. Assuming you do what is asked of you, for example the readings, and engaging with your classmates, for the units studied, then you can expect to get a passing grade.

And if you want to exceed this? Well do extra reading. As I already mentioned, pay attention to the journals. Don't be afraid to read too much, or do too much research…

Near the end of my degree, I remember somebody told me, that undergraduate work is only supposed to present, and deal with the knowledge already out there, and it is only when you reach the peak of postgraduate (masters and doctorate level) research, that these engaged minds are hoped to create new knowledge…

Yet when I was studying for this degree, every essay I submitted, especially for the final year modules, were novel ideas.

Facing an unknown horizon. And I really loved reading these challenging new texts; from Apartheid era African drama, to powerful Shakespeare, to founding Feminist Education ideas to an engaging third year Sociological class discussion. Which all really tried to put a hundred per cent in. And developed my reader's voice, to create new ideas never been previously known. I hope so anyway.

By staying with me so far, I hope you have come to value my way with words, which I took to my essays. So, whilst it is true at school, they may teach us to write in the third person to stay objective…

I still used the first person (stream of narrative), to carry off my essays off. And whilst I only hit the sixty eighth percentile for my final dissertation, which was disappointing because I was hoping to get a first (which is seventy percent or above). On reading it back, I noticed a few spelling errors, which will be what stopped me from getting the best grade. I should have listened to my supervisors who told me to proofread the darn thing! Oops.

I was still over the moon to graduate…

Most undergraduate degrees take three years, with the exceptions for Law or Medicine, which take more. However, my degree took extra time, partially because I did a blended study (of part time, and full time). And partly because I had to take extra units, to cover the fact that in my second year, I had switched to doing a combined program, of Theatre Studies, on top of my Sociology major.

The experience on completion has been one of intellectual wealth. And financial poverty. I am very pleased that I met the people I did meet, across the time. Had the conversations I had and read the books I read. But I am still paying off the debt I owe. Which has now breached twenty-five thousand!

You should be warned that you might meet the odd lecturer or two that you don't get on with. Academic doctors who, despite your best efforts, only give you passing grades for their units. I sure had a couple on my program. And it is a shame that people like this, still get lecturing roles, today, when if a student, puts his or her whole into his work, this study should be respected.

But don't let them get you down. Life is not always meant to be easy. We are set these obstacles to test us. If you can continue to do your readings and research, continue to engage with the work you are set, and continue to give it your all, you should hopefully have enough decent grades to carry you through to a good grade overall.

So yes, your degree will be a challenge, it will test you. Don't think that the somewhat inviting work you ease through in your first year, will continue in the second and third. Without shifting up gears. The work does get harder, and you will soon need to learn to up your game, to succeed. But don't let this defeat you.

If you keep up with the readings, and the in class and out of class discussions and subject engagement, you should do just fine. We develop as thinkers and readers, and the process is a rewarding one, if you stick with it…

I have given you some tips in today's entry, on how you can prepare, and ultimately complete your degree, with as best as I can. So, whilst it will be true that every degree is different, whether it is your sole aim to get a good job, perhaps in teaching, or another profession, don't let the workload overwhelm you. Don't give up, even if it seems like you can't get a good grade, even if you must retake a unit or two. Persevere forwards. I will be right there beside you on graduation.

10 : Insomnia

So, what do you want to talk about today?
I've got to be careful.

I'm holding on to some things, whilst still trying to get out every day.

I still like listening to music and playing on my games. Even if I must be careful that they don't take over.

I was able to get voluntary work, after I finished my degree. Although that packed up after six months. And I have had more than a few driving lessons, although I decided to hand in my provisional license after my latest admission into hospital.

God, I hate those places. It's like every time I go in, they keep me for years at a time. And that's no lie.

I go in, and I see other people go in and leave. Again, and again, and again and again. These people will enter and leave, and I will still be there. Silly idiots. How do they want me to forgive them for this? It's almost as if they think I am a risk to the world, whereas I am under the impression that all these medications they give me, only makes the problems worse and not better.

I can't prove this, but there we are. I don't like it how they say I am going to have to take them for the rest of my life. I don't like that at all.

So, what are the side effects, apart from putting on weight? Well it kills my sex drive. Which is proved by the fact that when I come off them, I am like a wild tiger, damn.

And what else? It slows down my speech. Again, when drug free, I speak faster. What else? They make me like a zombie. They reduce my strength and decrease my motivation for getting out. Hell, I used to walk everywhere, but now I can't be bothered to.

And they cause sleep disturbances. Something like insomnia. So that I must be careful not to be up in the nights, and in bed at day. This could be down to a poor routine, and I can fight it by getting up on time and going to bed at reasonable hours. Yet even this seems to be a struggle.

I love my sleep. But it is rare for me to get to bed before midnight even if I want to. Sometimes, I go to bed early, then wake up when it is still dark, unable to get again to sleep. So, the poor cycle continues.

I didn't lie on my benefits application form. I do have problems with engaging with people. And I also have other 'life' problems, which persist despite me being out of hospital. If anything, they continue, because of this.

11 : Progression

It was a big step for me, to escape those golden walls, and return to a space I can call my own. I used to like playing my games. On the Xbox One, and I still do. That alongside with meeting my dad, wife, and other friends. And listening to the music, I don't really have that much time left over.
It's like how my consultant wants me to get another General Practitioner. Yet I haven't done so. I told him, "I am too busy". So, he responded "Busy doing what?"" Watching YouTube music videos?" "Yep" I answered.

Curse them. Who do they think they are? Hell, what has a

General Practitioner ever done for me? Apart from pretend to shake my hand, and give me a fake smile, whilst they pretend to listen to my rants.

What do they want me to do? You know every time I enter hospital, it takes a General Practitioner's signature, as well as a social worker's, and a consultant. It's bull-crap.

I know as much about my own health as they do. If these guys were so smart, then they would have 'fixed' me, within a few weeks of admission, instead of keeping me on and on.

The same goes for the consultants, damn them. I wouldn't even have one of these, if given the chance. I have learned about the 'rule of thirds', which is one third of inpatient admissions, will only have a brief stay, and then get out and get better. Another third will be admitted then get out and eventually get better. This will take longer, but they will do it, nevertheless. And the remaining third, will remain on drugs and sick, for the rest of their life. With only medication keeping them, 'well'. My community nurse tells me that I have already fallen into this 'worse' category, by the evidence of my long-term stays.

These professionals keep me in locked wards and don't like the fact that I know more about my own mental health than them. In this case why is it that when they give little privileges such as the ability to leave the ward, as a first step, and then the ability to take myself to town, and eventually have leave to sleep at my own flat, that I'm able to make much better progress and recovery, then when I'm trapped on those damn wards day after day? It stands to reason that the little exercise and fresh air, associated with this extra freedom a section seventeen brings, will of course be much better from me, than being trapped in that stupid cage!

These are things that belong to God. Not man. Not a man who thinks himself God. Not any doctors, or professionals, who think themselves, the warders of men. Damn them. They've never been my guardians. Prison guards, sure. They know how to lock the ward's doors when I am inside them.

They even supervised the theft of my laptop, which held lots of valuable, and pretty much irreplaceable chess lessons, as well as the original digital copies of my books. These guys took that. Or at least one of the patients on the ward took it, and one of the nurses co-opted with them to ensure they got the computer off the building. Not to mention my mail was repeatedly opened and the credit/debit cards stolen, along with the pin numbers, and I lost thousands from the accounts in this way!

Damn them.

I'm not saying that my writings, were good enough, to be published at the stage of first draft, they were when he took it. But that isn't the point. So, when quite recently, I tried to buy some advertising for their documents, the payments were rejected. One said it was because I didn't have the book title on the cover, but the other didn't even have a decent reason. Which for all we know is because the content has already been published elsewhere.

In fact, believe it or not, but I once found a significant portion of my first book, in another famous author's novel. Stephen King I think it was. And we are talking word for word plagiarism here. This was for 'JoJo's Amazing Adventure and other short stories. Of course, I would hardly be able to claim copyright over it because that guy has millions and would beat me in any court case. I also know how he got hold of the manuscript (that first draft I sent to a scandalous so called publishing company, and the contact I had over there said he never received the memory stick I had posted to America, only an open, empty envelope).

So, this is how the document was stolen, and later copied, most likely sold to Mr King, for God knows how much?

So, what next? Hopefully I will be able to continue working at this book/novel, for such a time as will be enough for a reader to engage and swim with it. New ideas, suggestions, and currents, carrying me along. With my own life's journey being upheld within these windows of pages. Like mirrors, they can catch the light, as well as moments, to a decent progression and conclusion. Finishing when the natural progression of this narrative reaches its close.

12

The police detective didn't look amused

…

"Okay JoJo so what do you want to talk about today?
Your crimes?

….

"No but you've already signed the waiver?! This is out of your hands…

…

"What have you done which is so special? What have you achieved that makes you *so* good, that you think anyone will want to read?

"Talking about Ninjas? Ha!
How can you be a Ninja, when you can't even walk three steps without wheezing for breath?

"Or computer games? No man come on, that stuff is for children!

"What makes your little world so compelling, that it will have dreams any higher than the average man. Or woman now we come to think of it?

"So, what, you have read some powerful authors in your past.

"That doesn't give *you* any precedent!

"If you want to be original, and I very much hope you do, you're going to need to start knocking down some of the walls, which you have erected, to reveal areas of your life, that you have previously kept standing.
"And you can't do that? So how are you going to write a bestselling novel?

"Sorry what was that? You say, *everyone* has limits?
"Like teachers *can't* teach outside the curriculum.
"Or lawyers *can't* discuss their other client's cases, with others, without betraying their confidence?

"Or how surgeons and doctors, *must*, uphold the Hippocratic oath, in their actions on graduation, to do no harm, and serve the best of their ability, to the welfare of patients universally?
"Not to mental patient confidentiality?
"You mean that? How a soldier, must obey orders, or face court martial?
"Is that what you mean?

"You really think you can write a whole novel, off the back of your subconscious leftover raggedy mind and subliminal *souvenir* base. (Which means *memory* in French. ed)

....

"What gives you that impression?
What gives you that right?

…………………

"So, you have written before, yeah,
I get that….
"I see that you have got a degree, a
good one for what it's worth. Well
done. Many people don't have.
"What seems to make you think
that your grade, is somehow
superior to those others who don't
have this?
"That you brought your bride over
from another country. Good for
you.
"Shame you couldn't hold on to
her for more than a few years, here
in this country….
"That you are so sick, that you are
forced to take an injection every
month, for what would seem like

the rest of your life. Good for you.
"How does this change things, in
any little way?
"In fact, how is a mental illness
something to be proud of?

"Unlike the other people, who get
sick, take meds, then get well and
come off them. You have been on
these medications for Fifteen years
now, and there is a good chance
that you will never get off them.
"Yes, I know it is your intention to
break free of this choke hold, but
really? When every other time you
have come off them you end up
relapsing...
"I know the social predicaments,
not to mention interpersonal ones,
have troubled you in the past at the
same time as your breakdowns.
"But the fact that you have now

spent over five years on locked wards, means that the odds are stacked against you I'm afraid. "Other people get it, get better, and get off their drugs? Yet you get bad and go downhill way too fast. "Every-time.

"And so, what, you met a senior police chief in town, a couple of decades ago, who offered you a job in the police, for you to turn it down, without due consideration? "Even if I were to believe that this did happen, despite your protestations, how does this give you any head room? You didn't take the job; you didn't get the promotion. You haven't done it?

"You what? You lost what? To whom? Taking how long? Sex you

say. What is that? I can barely remember. And it doesn't matter? Suit yourself. Seems like with the rest of the world you are preoccupied, so how does this somehow make you an exception? ....

"And you are holding on to what? With whom? What oaths are you striving to respect when you already broke them a long time ago?

"JoJo. JoJo. JOJO! Listen to me kid. You are a joke. Your entire life is built on a Vernier of falsehoods and misinformation.
"You are a *keyboard* warrior. You think that just because this book, has taken a kick-off from your many thousands of failed, online

appearances, that this digital fame somehow crosses over, to the real world? Well let me assure you son, that it doesn't.

"Why do you think it is you can't get a job? Why is it do you think that you are still many thousands in debt £££ to these credit card companies?

"Come off it our kid. You really think that level of debt, is an accolade not baggage?
Where are you going? You live alone. You suffer cycles of delusion, and stupid relationships with people you have met, and are probably never going to see again.

"You think that this world is the only one?

You think that we don't have to
pay for our actions?
That your child is not going to miss
you when you go?
That the world will not be a better
place, when your miserable
specimen, stops leaching off the
state, and the state provided
National Health Service?

"Come on our kid.
Start taking responsibility for your
actions.

"For all those people you have hurt
with your actions, all this needs to
be answered.
You thought you were the centre of
the world.
And then you made up some lame
excuse, that at the centre, is the
pivot. On which the rest of the

world rotates. You struggled to get your degree. And then when you finally got it, you struggled to do anything with it.

"So, you finally say, that you have set the imprint, lit the touch paper, for your daughter, to walk.
Opened the door, for a child, to walk through. And you think that this is going to be any easier for her when she grows up?
That she won't have to face the face hurdles and barriers, in her transition, to adulthood, that you are undertaking, just because you have been there yourself?

"You think somehow that her life will be easier, just because yours was hard?

"Hard life? Don't make me laugh. All you do is sit on your bum all day and drink coffee in town? What is so hard about that?

"Who cares that you didn't have any friends at school? Who cares that you failed at Physical Education?
"Who cares that every partner you have ever had, has walked away from you, rather than be dragged down by your self-pity and commiseration?

"Who cares man? Not us…

"So how about I start putting some ticks in boxes, whilst your story remains unfinished?

"A downwards trajectory. Your crimes are such, that it is going to be impossible to ever see any future meaningful employment. And so, what you have joined a gym? All you are doing is adding stress to that already shattered heart."

"And my child, what about her?" JoJo whispered.

"Sure, we all hope that she does well. Hope that she makes something of her life, that she can graduate, and that you will be there to clap on her graduation, the same as she was there for yours.

"But don't think that she won't have to walk through the barrier. Walk the pit of fire, which scars as it does whittle down the numbers of those who can, to those who cannot.

"And her accolades, and achievements, will be hers alone. We can't take away from one another's victories but must build on our own. And this goes to everybody from the future king of England, to the lowliest beggar on the street. God help them.

"An intergalactic game of chess. This is fifty shades of ember. Real life with real people you are playing with, real hands, minds and hearts. Just because your body works like a zombie doesn't give you the right to drag down everyone else around you…

"Please take a step back now and let others with their whole lives ahead of them, take precedence in the roles you were unable to see through.

"A Forty year old man, with no car, no house, and no job. And for the time being at least, no wife and daughter! Things are not looking good, are they?"

JoJo said nothing

13 : Martial Art

Okay. I want to get thematic for a bit. Let us talk about martial arts? So where does my training and knowledge come from?

    I first studied Judo at secondary school. I didn't rank up

at this point. For the two Judo gradings I should have gone to and passed, I flunked out of both. Calling sickies. Which was a bit lame, but then seeing as my secondary school education was just that, lame, then why should Judo have taken me above this?

But I did learn two things from these lessons. Firstly, how to 'break-fall', which is how to fall, or take a throw, and prevent yourself from damage on the landing. Which is very important in martial arts? This applies to any fight, where you stand a chance of being thrown.

How you do it, does depend on the attack, but the basic premise is this : You cast your hand and arm out to the floor, before you meet it, ahead, so that on the impact, your upper limb, takes the force of the impact fall.

You must ask yourself as the opponent, which would you rather, be hit by a strike, or be hit by the world, which is what's going to happen by a throw. Also, should you find yourself in a position of attack, against a single adversary, having the power of Judo, which is control, throw and pin, is a very effective repertoire. I'm not saying you can step into the Octagon, and start winning Championships, with this single repertoire alone. But for the 'street' and self-defence in a real-life confrontation, it is very good.

What else? Well the second thing I learned from these classes, was the act of communion. Something, I was never able to properly capitalize on, in my youth. And it wasn't until my adult hood, hospital and then university life, that I was properly able to demonstrate and build on this knowledge. But the simple act of being in a training hall, with other likeminded learners, and to learn, listen, build, and develop, is so important for me. And for the next generation, which is why schools and teaching are so important. I really take my hats off to teachers their job is so important and building up the knowledge and confidence of the next generations, remains one of the most important foundations our society has to offer.

.....

I have of course learned other important martial lessons across my life. So much so that my second (A Patient in Time : JoJutsu) and third books (Fighting Madness), take prime position in staking this claim, and building a foundation for my martial world.

It seems to be that the internet, now so heavily guarded and moderated, that anything that senses novelty and originality, and steps outside of the norm, is heavily cast out too easily in my opinion. It seems to be very difficult to create something new, in this world where who has the biggest wallet, seems to take precedence over everything else. That's not to say that you, as a newcomer, don't have a chance to make it in this world.

Sign up to your local dojo, be it Tae-Kwon-Do, Judo, Karate, Kung Fu, Aikido, Kickboxing, Boxing, Gracie Jiujitsu, Judo or Jeet-Kun-Do. Just be warned that ego and pride in martial arts, seem to be heavy. The odds are that your sensei/master/or teacher, will expect you to honour and bow down to him (or her), from the get-go.

They want you to do well, but to conform, and if you do step out of line, or use your martial knowledge outside of the dojo/ring, don't expect more than one warning before being kicked out of the club. This is my experience of it anyhow.

So, what now? You can continue to learn from outside the ring. When you have conflicts with your opponent's/enemies in real life, it is good to have the knowledge that you can defeat them in fisty cuffs, should things reach that stage. Obviously, you want to avoid this from happening. The same as your goal should be to walk away from confrontations before they arise. Or let the professionals/police etc. deal with the worst situations before you must. But it is good to have some knowledge, and direct powers, to fall back on, should the need arise.

So, what other moves to I know? Well probably the next move I have in my arsenal is Ikkyo. Which to sidestep, and then swipe, the enemies attack. I first learned this from my aunties' boyfriend Danny when I was still living at my mum's house about the year two thousand. Danny was a high black belt in his own style of Karate, which he had several dojos opened in his unique style of Karate, across Britain and Ireland and Africa. Danny taught me Ikkyo, part of how to escape a grip. Any grip will always take place in one of four ways. On top, thumb under. Or on top thumb over. And then under thumb over, or thumb and fingers over. This may be difficult to visualise, but if you can get a friend to grab your arm or wrist, and you should be able to practice these moves for yourself.

The breakaway Danny taught me, uses the knowledge, that the thumbs, are the weak point of a grip. And then, when attacked in this way, you can pull your hand free, using the other hand, and an awareness of the grip. Or even simply by twisting your offended arm, in face of this first digit, skill and movement, will enable you to escape, without even needing to use the second arm.

Should however you be grabbed by both arms, then to my knowledge, you will need to use both arms to generate the power of the breakaway needed. Depending on the strength of your adversary of course.

So, what else do I know? Well homage to the late grandmaster sifu Bruce Lee, I've got his one-inch punch down to a par as well. I even did a YouTube video of this at one point, although I think I've since taken this down. And we are taught in Aikido never to attack, at least never to be the aggressor. But this move, the one-inch punch, was something I skilled in, before Aikido. And literally is another skill. I developed this, by punching walls, be it in a police officer holding cell, or outside. And again, this is not something to be taken lightly, and I have also never been told to do this voluntarily.

I think there is a whole martial world dedicated to throwing, and receiving punches, namely Boxing, and Kick Boxing, both of which I only have limited knowledge of. When you develop as a martial artist, and when you develop your own experience and skill range. You will be opening doors. So that, should the occasion arise that you are forced to defend yourself, you will have choices, options on how to react. Throwing a punch, or an Atemi, can be one of these.

Something else I would like to mention, another facet of my martial repertoire is footwork. Watching the placement of the steps of your opponent, can tell you a great deal. And this is best practiced, not so much in the ring, as it is from walking locations, from A to B.

I realize that as we grow older, and hopefully procure and later master use of the four wheels (driving), many people get out of the habit of excessive walking. But don't become so lazy that you never walk anywhere. Because footwork, in fights, and conflict situations especially, is very important in telling you, how your opponent intends to act, and how best you can position yourself to react against him. Or her, should you be a woman fighting a woman.

What else? I also want to stress the importance of DVDs and books. Whilst it is an ideal to train in a dojo, with others. And to develop yourself for competitions, should the opportunity arise. It is also good to read and watch others, from the static media, on the occasions that you can't attend class in person. Or even as well as. I will aim to create a list, with some brief descriptions, or martial arts books I have read and can wholeheartedly recommend, at the end of this book, so you can take heed from these, should you so desire.

I think that draws to a close this brief if important lecture for today. There is much more I know about this field, but it is quite hard to summarize, and capture in written form, without freezing up. Or running dry.

The world of martial arts and discipline is such a vast one, and indeed one which I have only touched in my life, as well. But respect and discipline, are the key concepts you should honour, in your practice of it.

There is a term called Budo, which means 'The Martial Way', this is something that all martial arts clubs, I've ever been a part of, respect and seek to honour. The one's I've been allowed to join that is at least!

In their practice, and teachings. To honour your teacher/ sensei/ sifu/ master, to honour your style, and your family, your community, your country, and ultimately to honour man (and woman) kind!

So be punctual for your classes, trim your nails, and stretch before classes and so on. Good luck.

14 : Stopping smoking and a fight

Okay. I've done what I said I was going to do. Read a few chapters of the brilliant book *Easy way (by Allen Carr)*. And you know what? Yes, it has helped me stop cigarettes. By carefully walking down the path he narrates for us, I now feel comfortable in the safe role on non-smoker, again.

I need to be careful. No more, picking up the nub ends off the floor. No more urges for the odd pack or smoke. This is my health, and future we are talking about here. I have gone about two weeks now I think, without a cigarette. If anything, I owe it to my daughter, to stay off them.

So, what else? Last night I got in to a 'fight'. With one of my mates. Even though it was less a fight, then randori, which is a controlled battle/bout, between two willing opponents. Like we agreed, beforehand, to stop whenever one of us asked.

And I already had it in my mind, that I wasn't going to hurt him. I didn't want to throw any blows, merely control him, and maybe get into the clinch.

Well what happened, is that I grabbed him, and held on to him. He escaped, but then I was able to grab him again. I ended up ripping his coat, and I ripped it worse the second time I grabbed him. I think it was my coat he had stolen off me anyway, in the first place. So, I don't feel too bad about mashing it. Even though I did offer to buy him a McDonald's to make up for this. And don't mind buying my friend a meal.

So, what else then? Did I tell you that yesterday I got pinked, and then banned, from one of the martial arts websites, I used to be a member of. I have a big problem with them doing this to me.

Despite what my dad says (that the internet is full of nonsense, and is only bad news for me), I did used to enjoy logging on to this site. And chatting and laughing with my friends there. And so yeah, I was upset when they banned me, for what must be the fourth time from there.

But I've no intention of going back there. It is unfair what they've done, to pink me (which is a temporary withhold of posting privileges), followed by an outright ban within twenty-four hours, and no spark point, or reason, to trigger this. Damn.

I need to switch my lifestyle from a night stalker, to one who walks in the light. Or in other words, to start getting up at decent hours. But it's hard. Once you get caught in the trap of going to bed late, then even if you want to go to bed early, the body fights it.

And even if in some ways I am strong willed, such as able to complete a degree, and not miss any lessons due to sleeping in, that was hard. Now I am past that 'hard' part of my life, I am not in any rush to force myself up every day. There just seems to be no need.

These days, I also must get up for my injections, once a month, at the hospital. I normally must be there for ten thirty AM, and sometimes my dad gives me a lift in, so that helps that. But I still struggle, and I need to sort it out, so I can restore some sort of normality visiting my immediate family, which I can't do when I am asleep all day. To be continued…

15 :

"So, JoJo", the police constable continued,
"We heard you have been getting in to fights again. This is not good. This is looked down upon. You do realize that we now, as a school, conduct a zero-tolerance policy to fighting. Do you really think that your borderline knowledge of martial arts gives you a license to fight? A license to harm, a license to kill.

Because it does not. If anything, that yellow belt should have taught you about discipline, restraint. Instead you act like a bull in a china shop. Bullying these poor hapless individuals before you. And if any one of them should ever stand in your path? Ever say no, well god help them!"

……

"Let me ask you a question… Can you please tell me about that list you drew up a few years ago? You know the one you wrote when you were severely unwell? Very psychotic?
I heard it was a list of your enemies. And a random selection of their friends on the internet? I heard it offered rewards, bounties on their heads. That you contacted 'Anonymous', and with your rudimentary knowledge of computer and hacking skills, ordered their execution. That some

of them went in to hiding, and that some of them were terminated?"

"Do you really consider this a good use of the stock market funds? To execute random people, who some little troll gets upset by? You call yourself a sniper? Then you use an AK-50 in a crowded room. With the doors and windows barred. So that some of them must go in to hiding. And not everyone makes it out alive.

What gives you the license to conduct this kind of operation? You say it was you against the world? You say you didn't like their attitude towards you? You said that they would pay for what they did to you?

And we tried to order your assassination. Sent a message to an operative, giving them your description, and executing the target? Except it didn't work! Instead the message was relayed to your address, giving you pre-emptive knowledge of the strike, and a wariness which allowed you to call it off?

Or maybe it wasn't your power which cancelled this order, but we considered your circumstances, the good will and support you have showed in looking after your daughter and wife, and decided that you could do more good alive, then dead.

That your head will help more on top of your body, than off it?

You do know that you are on your final warning. And that if you ever consider it right to break the rules again, we won't hesitate to act. And this time the two years you last spent in detention, will seem like a walk in the park.

You have been warned!"

16 :

Relax, survive, and get better.
Okay guys and girls, youth, and elders. Take your time. This is your adventure, your journey.
It's not a race. Even if sometimes, you will need to win your own battles.

Listen to your own songs. Make your own relationships. You can't win every battle. You can't win every fight, without taking a blow or two. Losing a cut or two, a scrape or two.

The world is changing. Back in the day, not everyone would smile. In photographs. I was one of the first to smile.

I remember posing for a police mugshot, and then smiling for the camera. Nearly all the perps who get their profile's taken didn't smile. But when they took mine, I made my grin from ear to ear. Funny really. Laughing out loud.

I have started reading a new book. *Sacred contracts* by *Caroline Myss*. She talks about the religious founding fathers, Abraham, Jesus, Mohammed, and the Buddha. She says that these powerful people, each initiated, and fulfilled their heavenly contracts, starting in their late twenties, but then realized coming on to their thirties.

People have different trajectories. Must go through their own battles. Different levels of knowledge, Sophic gnosis. Learned from the Christian Goddess, Sophia.

So, what now? Relax. Survive. Get better. I am under the impression that these medications I'm on, kind of make me into a zombie.

When I saw, one of my good friends a few days ago, she said that she thought that I was very unwell. But when I have seen my professionals recently (mental health nurses and consultant), they all said how much better I looked.

I guess it's all relative. My friend maybe hasn't seen much of me since I have come out of hospital ten months ago. So, she doesn't have an accurate base to judge me off. Maybe that, or maybe now I am quite unwell. When I look in the mirror, I see big black lines under my eyes.

At least I have stopped watching porn on my computer. That stuff rots the mind.

So, what else? I'm struggling with this stop smoking thing. I haven't had a cigarette in about a month. But I'm on the vape stick. Which provides me with lots of replacement Nicotine. I would give this up as well, except I'm not strong enough too. One day hopefully. I'm also finding it hard to get the energy to walk into the town. The buses from my local stop are so regular, it is hard not to hop on the bus with my gold card, at every opportunity.

I think when I next have my medications reduced, if they are that is, I will get some energy back. Get some powers back. Get my appetite back. Have my insomnia, and sleeping routing improved. Able to focus better on games better.

Give up smoking better. Also get my sex drive back better. I don't know what they are putting in these drugs. But I am sure part of it is a medical castration. Don't forget that the last time, I got out of hospital, I was able to go wild with my Johnson, and then I also spent lots of money, on my credit cards on hookers. Now I am in debt. So, I just must stay on top of these, pay off my debts. And take it easy.

Good luck!

17 : Desperate

Yeah so there we were. She had left me, and I was desperate. Talking to the strangers on the street. Smoking drugs. And somebody knocked me out.

"Wow, that must have hurt?" Yeah, it's kind of did. Do you want to know the story?

"Sure, go on."

So, there I was on the streets of Derby litter picking. A useful skill I learned from my secondary school days.

Anyway, I came across a broken Budweiser bottle, on the street, next to a bus stop. And I was picking up the bits of glass. Then this big black guy came up to me and kicked it out of my hands.

I shouted "Oi" and "What do you think you are doing?"

And I can't remember what he said. If he said anything at all? Only then I started picking up the glass again. And by this time, my hands were covered in cuts, from the glass.

Then like a real idiot he came up and kicked the bag out of my hands again. This time rather than attempting to diffuse the situation verbally, I went up to him and pushed him on the chest.
Big mistake. In a flash he sparked me out, (he punched me hard in the head, enough to knock me clean out).

I might have survived the punch, had it been daytime. But because it was midnight, and pitch-black, I was knocked out cold.

Some people told me, when I was in hospitals after this, that I should have ducked. But I wasn't ready. And he got me.
Anyway, I woke up in an ambulance, and a police officer told me that they have him in the back of a meat wagon (police car), and asked me if I wanted to press charges…

A beat…

I considered it but told them that I didn't. Told them to let him go.
He probably deserved a criminal record for what he did to me. But I'm not a grass. Plus, you could well argue *I deserved it.*

Anyway, they took me to hospital, and I waited on a hospital bed, with the live Emergency Room taking place around me. And then I walked out. Because I don't like hospitals. And it's not like there was anything they could have done for me.

I went back to a friend's house, but she turned me away. Then I went to my dad's place, and he called an emergency psychiatric assessment on me, where they unanimously agreed to have me sectioned, from July 2017 to October 2018, two years. I think I must hold the record for lengthy inpatient stays in hospital. In the UK anyway.
Anyway, the professionals took one look at me and put me on a section three

(six months) no messing about! So whilst most people only do a *week or two* in there, I did nearly *three years!* And it wasn't the first time. Damn.

Well we need to look at the positives. So at least when I left, I had managed to procure a nice new flat, in a new part of my hometown, Derby. And I have also applied, and been accepted for, a decent amount of monthly benefits. Which I fully deserve, seeing as the state owes me this, given the amount of time I did locked away. I even spent six months of my admission, in Bradford. Which was difficult, seeing as I was a smoker again, by this point, and in Bradford, on the acute ward, you weren't allowed any cigarettes, then on the less acute ward, we could have two a day, for most of the time. And I think this may have been upped to four a day, by the end. But it is so different, between having your freedom, and being restrained to the will of others.

Therefore, I harbour such amount of hatred for certain people. Such as my dad, and my community nurse, and the various consultants. Because these were the people, who were responsible for my detention, and I find it hard forgiving them for this.

They still treat me like a little boy, even though I am thirty-eight. Where has my life gone? But at least I have a family, which includes my daughter. And they mean the world to me. Many people go through life, without ever having been able to hold on to what I have…

Whilst it is true, that I haven't been able to hold down a job, or a career, and my degree, I am now in a nice flat with weekly meetings with my stepdaughter. And if I have learned one thing from doing it, that's how to do a degree. So, know if my children want to do one, which I can recommend, and I can also support them through it. Something my parents hardly ever did for me.

When I was a child, I didn't really have any friends at school. And when I got my GCSEs, I really couldn't see a future. In hindsight, I should have gone to college, and made friends there. But hindsight is a fine thing. Which means that, unless others can share this knowledge with us, we must learn the hard lessons in life ourselves. Learn the hard way.

I did eventually go to college, four different colleges in fact. As the years rolled by.

And in 2005 I faced my first admission for mental health. It was messed up. I have been in and out of hospital for many times, since then. It's 2019. But I shouldn't be hateful. I have got a loving separated wife, and daughter. Who I love to the ends of the Earth, and I don't need anyone more now that I have got these two?

I don't really talk about them too much because it is private information. And none of your business. But they are the yin to my yang, and I still value their input tremendously in my life, especially now that I have my freedom back, and can see both on a regular basis.

18 : Never forget this

Take a big breath. And let us take a step back…
"Where are we going today?" Ren inquired.
"I want us to move forwards… and I want us to move backwards…!" JoJo provided.
"But how is that possible, JoJo".
Ren was stumped. This perplexing oxymoron sent the Ninja's head spinning.
"By the power of the spoken word" JoJo suggested. "Don't be worried about time. We are going

older; this happens every day. But those books of mine you discarded…"

"Yes, what of them?"
"I want us to revive them, to remind them. Those epic fables, of Chinese and Indian parables, let's hold on to them?"
"So, you want to rewrite them?" Ren inquired.
"Maybe. But let us just hold on to the past. This younger generation, the Millennials, where would they be without the building blocks our ancestors provided for us?"
"What building blocks?" Ren was still stumped.
"Ever heard of the French revolution? Where the generation of the future, discarded the old (ancient) regime of the past?"
"Um hmm".

"Or how about the pyramids, those giant miracles of achievement".

"I'm not here to trick you Ren. I want us to work on these projects together. Like we did before".

"Just like the good old times?"

"Just like the good old times."

So how do we start the stories, where does it begin?

It begins with a young child called JoJo. JoJo was exceptional, for what he was not. Bands made songs laughing at his name. And when he sat down to write his first book, all he could think about was stealing!

"Really, that's quite a poor excuse to write!"

"I know" JoJo scolded, but there we go.

"He also had dreams, dreamed of flying away to exotic countries, becoming a man, and bringing back his bride…"

"Wow, that sounds juicy", Ren lifted.

"So, did he ever succeed in this aspiration? or was he forever a stalker of the night?"

"A stalker of the night, night stalker? What the hell are you going on about Reynold?"

"Oh, I don't know".

"Anyway, back to our protégé, he wasn't a night stalker, whatever you meant by that confusing query. He was however an insomniac, and a menace. As a child he didn't have any, friends at school. Or at least none that would be able to save him from the black hole he was about to fell into."

"Then after completing his GCSEs, but before collecting the results he was hit by a car, crossing the road. From this he broke his neck, and was in a controlled, induced coma for ten days!"

"Wow, so he broke his neck. Wow he is lucky to be alive!"

"I know Ren. You're right."

"What happened next?"

"He started visiting the library and he found two books to love and cherish. He had not actually been able to do any reading in hospital, and so holding down the attention to finish these books he had found, was difficult at first. But he persevered and succeeded."

"So, what were these books about?" Ren continued.

"The first was a book of Indian short stories, and the second was a book called "Concentration and Meditation", by Christmas Humphreys".

"So where does the Chinese influence come from then?" Ren seemed unhappy, unsatisfied.

"Have you ever heard of Bruce Lee?"

"That epic Chinese martial artist? Wow, of course I have! Who hasn't? But where does he come into this narrative? I thought we were talking about your character?"

"I am Reynold. But hold on. I remember staying up late one

night, at my mum's house, and watching Bruce Lee's last complete, and epic film *Enter the Dragon*. And then walking a couple of miles to a park, at midnight. I don't know if I had a weapon with me, a Jo staff for example. I don't think I did. Only a hessian bag. Anyway, I walked this long distance to this park, near my local university, from which I would graduate from some twenty years later."

"JoJo", Ren took a deep breath. "But what has this got to do with writing?"

"Well" finished JoJo, "after watching his films, and fighting my own fear of walking long distances in the dark, I also brought Bruce's first complete book, 'The Tao of Jeet-Kun-Do'".

"And?"

"Well this martial arts Bible, suggested many of the moves, and power, that this character had. And was also close to my beginning footsteps, into the martial world. Not just the images, but the ideas. That one man can take on the world. Like he did, or Nelson Mandela, or Jimi Hendrix, or Mohamed Ali. Or Joan of Arc. Or John F. Kennedy!"

"Some powerful names you have cited there. And so, from this vacuum you were able to find inspiration, and direction?"

"Something like that".

"The powerful heroes of the past, as well as the known, and some unseen heroes of the present, have protected your life, ever since the day you died. And whilst you still have problems, you need to see each day as a blessing, hold on to the treasures that your friends and family give you every day. Say thank you for these blessings, and everyday do your best to make the world that little bit better. This is your responsibility as a son, husband, and father. Please never forget it!"

19 : Moving forwards

JoJo took a rest.
Who was he?
Ren took a rest. Who was he? He was JoJo's friend. He took a ride with him. He followed him over the mountains. Read his books.

Listened to his music. Accepted his mistakes and visited him when he was in hospital.

This life isn't always easy. Sometimes the devil throws sin at us. Smoking cigarettes, drinking beer, and watching porn.
We need to try and cut down on these errors. Cut down on our sins and build an acceptable life. And if we don't? Then Karma will hit us in the ass.

We need to love our families, our partners, our children, our friends, neighbours, communities. And lastly our enemies.

Drink coke. Drink coffee. Drink milk. I don't know what else to say.

Try to write. Write essays, write books. Build networks.

Speak languages. Build a life, with what you've got, not what is presently inaccessible to you! What else?

JoJo has a history. Not always positive, and he doesn't know if he can undo the damage that he's done. But he is trying.

20 : A Glimpse of Games

Sit down. Calm down. We all know why you are here. That's not the problem. This isn't just about you. It's about us. What can we achieve?
The world has changed. Forget 9/11 and 7/7 It is no longer Goliath against Samson. Too many tears have been shed. Too many lives have been wasted.

So, here's the deal. You work
with me, and I will work with you.
You work for me, and you will get
paid.

You look after your family,
and I will look after you.

You revise the texts, your
texts. And I promise I will read
them.

Damn right they don't make music
like this any-more.

Good old Shadow has rinsed
that gene pool for far too long, for
far too many innocents wrought.

There is no longer a thing
called good luck. The books have
been traced, and beggared, fixed,
for too many millions.

Walk your damn mile. The
hangman's isle. You did the crime;
you do the time. There is no such

thing as immortality, and if you cross us you will be dropped faster than a fat man toilet brick. And that's the nice way of saying it. There is a network. And viruses, spread faster than a stingray in the Galactus.

I don't care about your training. I don't care about your stimulus. This isn't then, this is now.

Take the internet. Break it. Put it back together again. Break it again. Fix it again. Break it, again. Fix it again.

Do we see a pattern arising here?
You know chess? Great play me. Prove it? You don't learn it. I will teach you.

You think you are good? Beat me... You want to lose to me?

Great, do so. The world is your oyster. Damn I learned that rubbish in school.

That and chatting up girls. Who I didn't stand a chance with? But I've made my quarter mill. Spent it. Now save it again!

Drive. Fly. Play. Lose. Win. Vote, abstain… Where are we going here?

I'm driving in the night, tonight. Proper ammunition. I'm down with the refugees.

And for all those criminals that steal our time? Damn you. Who do you think you are playing? God?

He only had one ring. On the ring finger? And his mother, Mother Mary? What about Mother Theresa?

Hey, you should I slow down? Nah kid drive fast. Just cos they got a badge they could still be imposters. Lyrics from the Fugees debut album the Score. They don't make em like that anymore. As I already stressed.

Do you know what I missed the most when I was in hospital for those long years?
Freedom? Yep. Freedom to walk to town. Yep that as well. How about fresh air?

But you know what. I've learned a lot from hospital. And it's not just been about chatting up the nurses. Although that did help.

Making friends. Engaging with different energy wavelengths. Eating different foods. Dining like a king, from a rationed menu base.

What else? You're not getting out. Not after what you've done. And when you do get out, if you ever do, we will keep you on such a tight leach that one slip up, one criminal misdemeanour and we will have you back in that cage faster than a fat man who sat down to fast. That's fatist. Lol

So where are we headed. Deep into the night. Across literature. Music, books, a glimpse of games. And on a very rare occasion, a movie. Now who would think that your best friend would be your worst enemy, and your enemy your best friend?

21 : Hacking

Calm down. Relax. You will pay
for your crimes. We all do. Karma
catches up with us in the end.
Do you want to know a skill, that I
failed to learn at school? Making
friends. I didn't learn that at
primary, and I did not learn it at
secondary. Do you know where I
learned it? I learned it in hospital.

    As the days rolled into
weeks, months, and now years…
Well at about the months stage,
there's only so much soul, and wall
gazing, that one can attend to,
before you must relate to the
residents. The guests. Guests of
honour. And no difference if you
will never see them again, you will
pick up medals along the way. My

life savers badge, which I got from saving a woman from the brink of death. She saw angels on her bed and went into cardiac arrest. So, I waited until to spasms stopped, before giving her mouth to mouth and chest compressions. But that's a different story.

So, these crooks, psychiatrists, and their minions, they can steal the best years of our life. But now that I have passed the halfway mark, of my 2054 destination, what do I have? What do I have to show for it?

A family? Check… Some internet friends. Check. A few books to my name, check.

What else? A portfolio, check. Which is growing by the quarter.

Martial arts? No. Not really. I have been bitten by one too many snakes, on my road to the next belt. It is a mainly misogynistic and ego driven world, that these black belts don't want to be driven off their horse. I'm not saying that it's all bad, just the ideas of rules, and martial laws, do as much to spit out, rather than engage with new ideas and people.

I've got my own style, my own movement! Which you would have known if you read my second book and third books!

So, what else. A couple of addictions, which I can't shake for the life of me. At least this time I seem to have got rid of my porn addiction. I can still visualize sex without having to watch it on the

screen each time I go to sleep.
Adult discretion advised.

With the help of the internet, I am
learning things about the C.I.A.,
John F Kennedy, and the Vietnam
and cold wars, that I never knew
before. I like hacking the systems,
because I am using my hacking
skills, first broke with Uplink (an
indie PC game of twenty years
ago), to give me special insight into
these missions, the game revolves
around. And it would be easy just
to say, "oh yeah, it's only a game,
all of that is make belief", which I
would be tempted to confer with, if
it wasn't for the fact, that these
computer files seem pretty legit.

The only part of that system I
haven't been able to crack so far is
the numbers. So, some of the

ciphers are letters (just strings of apparently random letters). However, cracking that is easy, all you must do is go out into the root directory, and type DECODE (followed by the letters of the cipher), and it will provide the message.

However for the numbers, and just one guy figured this out on the internet, you have to have a key to the cipher, specifically, some paragraphs, from one of JFK's books, which is on the desk of the woman who is questioning you in the opening cut scene.

Take good care.

22 : Zombies

It's all in your hands young Jo.

The past. The future. The present…
So, what you've made some
enemies? Play with fire, and you
will get burned.

Only this time, not this time.
You are going to live another three
score, give or take.

So, your alias, 2054, is that
when you are destined to live
until? What is the significance of
the numbers?

I'm not sure. I kind of
selected them because it seemed
apt at the time. And then some?

Or Chess, or Poker, or
Supercity? Or Tekken, or Call of
Duty, or Skyrim, or Grand Theft
Auto, or Black Ops Three?!?

Or two paracetamols to take
the edge off the pain. Even though
you're not in any pain.

How about your psychiatrist calling your dissertation bull crap, and publishing it in an academic journal?

Yeah that sounds about right. *'Damn him'*, that's what I say.

I hope he gets paid enough money, to say that kind of stuff. Where's the gratitude, where's the sympathy. Oh yeah, sorry I forgot. This is the twenty first century, we don't have time for that nonsense out here.

Forget your crimes, forget your history. Forget the pedigree. This is the new world. Survival of the fittest. Like I said damn him. Damn the lot of them.

So, what else? Where do we go from here…? The other day one of my support workers, told me that he is reading one of my books (the second one, A Patient in Time), and he says that he thinks that I am a really good writer, he asked why I'm not writing any more…

That is positive thinking, and its people, and thoughts like that, that motivate me, to sit down, and write, like I am doing here. God bless him. You know who you are…

So, what else?

Anyway, eventually two of the guys died, but I held on. And the main man, even revived me four times. And I even revived him once, and so that was why he was being kind to me, I think? It was quite instructive watching this Alpha player

running like mad, from the masses
of the undead, as the level opened.
We killed lots of these undead.
And he had a nice and powerful
automatic rifle to do it with.
Eventually he died, and then it was
game over. But I think he got us to
level 24, which for those of you
knew to this Zombie Apocalypse,
is a worthy feat.

It is nice playing Call of Duty
Black Ops with my daughter, and
with other online enthusiasts, and
not bad for a game, which is
coming up to twenty years old. I
found that out today, by reading
the back of the box. To think of all
these years I have missed out, on
the visceral gore of the undead.
Mainly due to being locked up, for
reasons largely out of my hands.

But therein lies some other stories. And gives us ammunition for another day? Or another book? Or maybe I have already wept another about the past, in my four other books. We need to think of some new ideas, for this one, I dare say. Peace out.

23 : Do Not Jump to Conclusions

Time, control, and patience. Protect those you love. Attack those you hate. Try to find a happy medium between the two.

Like zombies for example. Put a bullet between their eyes. Make money.

Play games. Enjoy them. Watch other streamers, online, via YouTube or Mixer.

Take your time. Compose yourself. Eat. Exercise. Do Martial Arts, if you can find a dojo to enter, and a Sensei/master, who will train you. And doesn't take over their class with their gregarious ego.

Vape. And then one day switch to the Gum!

Don't drink, don't smoke. Try to avoid eating meat. Cook, do the laundry, hover, tidy, and wipe the table down. Make your bed. Wear fresh underwear every day. Pray. Meditate. Live a good life. Make good friends, on your journey to the grave.

Watch YouTube videos. Make your own streaming channel. If you care to? Watch others.

Have a family and look after them. Avoid unlicensed medications. I once thought they were the bee's knees, until I overdid it, and got burnt.

Don't pester the police, but contact them, if you think you are worried for your safety. Stay within the limits of the law. *Don't drink and drive.*

What else?

Study. Write. Write a journal, blogs, online chat, and your own book, if you can?

Take your time. Balance. Learn how to play chess. Learn the names of the pieces, their values, the three stages of the game. And how to convert an advantage (be it material, positional, or driven initiative) to a win. Take a draw, when offered, and you *don't* have a clear advantage.

Play Call of Duty Zombies. Black Ops 1 and 3, both have great zombie minigames. Kill zombies, before they kill you. But don't be afraid of dying. Because the zombies will kill you eventually. There are too many of them. Literally an unlimited supply. So, the zombies, will win in the end. They always do. Just be sure, you send a good number of them back to perma-death, the second time round!

Make good friends. Stay in touch with them. Make new friends but treasure the old. For they are silver, and these are gold.

This world is ours now! But be aware, we are going to someplace else after this one.

Repent your sins. You will not be in control anymore when this life is over.

Which direction you are heading to, up or down, well that is up to you. And don't think we live separate lives. We are all connected to one another. And our families, and our friends. And we are connected. Try to save yourself. And in the process, save one another.

Do not jump to conclusions. Let people have their say, let them say their side of the story.

Work if you can. Don't stress yourself out, over matters which are out of your hands. Write. Read. Listen. Talk, type.

That's all for today. Take it easy.

24 : JoJo's Confession

Back to the interrogation process :
"So, JoJo, if you mind me calling you that. Tell me some more about your crimes…"
     No comment

"Is it true that you killed someone?
Did someone over?
Acted inappropriately?
You know the longer you hold out, the worse it will be for you?
The longer you hold out, the worse it will get!?"

"Listen copper, I am not no snitch. And even if I did admit those crimes, I can barely remember any of them.

I've got assets now, and I'm not just talking about my bank balance"

"So, you wrecked the economy in two thousand and seven, and then again in two thousand and eight, both times when you fled to Africa, to seek the comfort in a love, you eventually realized? Is that it? Is that all you have to say for yourself?"

"Like I said, *bro*, you can't blame me for fleeing the U.K. My natural birthplace may be Manchester. But my original origin, the home of all of mankind is Eden. Read it on a map. The home of Adam and Eve. Eden East Africa Kenya!

God is our ultimate price, we all have to pay. And that's if you can even see him through the glow!?

"So, you think that you can make it to heaven, after what you've done. I doubt it. I doubt that very much!"

"Well officer, fortunately, it isn't down to you to decide my fate. This is a topic I have given some consideration. Because I believe, that just as the youth hold our future, so too does God hold our dominion. And if he has mercy, and a heart, which I sincerely believe he does, then how could an all-powerful, and omni present entity, allow the puny mortals of this life, face eternal damnation in the next? How could he?

I will tell you how… He couldn't. I'm not saying I don't believe in Hell. Sure, I do. But this whole, burn for eternity in damnation, sounds a bit too much old testament to me…

Because like I said, you can be saved. Sinners can repent. In this life, and maybe even in the next.

Jesus? Man. Son of God sure, but more than that, he was the son of man. He says this repeatedly in the Bible. His name is Jesus Christ, he is the son of man. Baptized by John. And they both paid the ultimate price. So was John's penalty for helping the Jews, and lighter than Jesus'. Is having your head removed from your shoulder's any easier way to go, than a crucifixion?

Or to be hung, go ask Saddam Hussein, about that one… The ultimate general, the ultimate war. Prove your manhood, by taking it out on a defenceless enemy. And look at the aftermath.

I've just offended Christians, Veterans, and others as well. But I've been honest. And So, help me Lord, if that's one thing I am good at that is my honesty.

I was even considering telling my consultant, when I next see him, of my crimes. I think I need to, just to get them off my chest. God help me, it will provide him with ammunition for my downfall.

Hopefully he won't do this, and I just pray that when I die, my name doesn't hit the press, in the worst possible way. Like it has for several creepy celebrities in recent years!

But for all the good people I have known in this life. Those who have known me at my best, and at my worst. Well I hope I have touched enough hearts, to leave space for one more in his almighty kingdom.

I do believe in multiple dimensions. My illness, at first a curse. But hold with it long enough, and it opens new doors, never imagined.

Like when I punched my dad smack bang in the face. Or shot him in the arm with an air rifle.

But then, I remember when he called all the doctors to his house, to carry out an emergency mental health act assessment, and have me committed for two years. Hell, that was tough. I'd say, along, with hitting the point three on the seven point scale of life signs, in my induced coma (which basically means I died), and sleeping rough for a few nights, and facing eternity in oblivion, when I faced divorce, or struggling with the mess of a five year degree, which I swear to god was another challenge. Or going through Primary and Secondary schools, without making any friends. Damn I've seen a lot.

So, what now? You want me to plead guilty?

Damn you. Damn you man. I will stand true to my God, my wife, and her children. That is what I am talking about. I will support them in their future and support every single man who has ever lost a loved one, and child, who has had to learn to survive on her own two feet. Or baby, that has leaned to speak, crawl, walk and smile.

We don't just live in this world. Our presence and being can be felt far above and below!"

25

Okay JoJo my brother. How about if I take you down a long journey. A journey with fifteen years behind you, and a good fifteen ahead. At least. A journey which has seen the

back of more than one good man
(I'm thinking scruffy Nick and Roy
the landlord here), and multiple
entrances into the mental health
system, with few outs. It's like a
game of poker (" All in"). Or chess
(" check, checkmate") And so on.
And so, you see, there is no one
way to do this.

Retain control of your sanity.
Stay in touch with your family.
Make good friends. Drop the bad
ones. There have been times when
I have needed such friends in my
life, when I had no one and I was
desperate to cling on to anyone I
could. Then I sought friendship
with some real nasty pieces of
work. Including a kid ten years my
junior, who robbed me blind, and
one ten years my senior, who
persuaded to me that he had seen

online videos of my wife, which
led to me ripping up my marriage
certificate. Scumbags both.

Anyway, what were we
saying? Oh yes, use your truths to
pronounce your story, as it appears
to your mind. There is no one right
or wrong way of writing your
book. Thousands, hell millions
have died in countless wars, from
World War Two, to Vietnam, to
Iraq, to give us the ability to speak
our minds and truths, to you the
reader, in this way!

We are built to fall in love
with one person. Yet in times of
passion, and loneliness, it is easy to
forget this fact. Try to remember.
Put the days of forgetfulness
behind you. We live in a universe
of parallel dimensions. Or space
time warps, or coloured reflections,

and shimmering forcefields. Or
Terabytes, and nano drops. Of new
friendships with old acquaintances,
and old memories with new
friends.

Time is not fixed. Victory is
determined by the winners, sure.
Yet he who is left standing, can
always have their voice heard.
Liars will lie. Are you ever a liar?
Have you ever lied? Do you
always tell the truth? I doubt it.
And if it is to protect the meek and
wards? Well more bravo you.

That responsibility which
starts with our loins, walks with us
down the aisle, on through
graduation, and on to our death
bed. Life is a not a right it's a
privilege. Don't count your
blessings when it's too late.

Say thanks every day. Thank you for the food on your plate, and the company you keep. Respect his knowledge and her body. Spend time with your friends. You never know when you might need them. One day, they will be taken away from us. All of them, one by one. So, hold on to what is good, whilst you still can.

JoJo out.

26 : What We Can Do for You?

"So, the next question JoJo is what can we do for you?"

"Restart contact with my wife and child?

Provide a regular income, with a bank balance remaining, to give to my loved ones, if I die?

Not beat me up, knock me out, or mean that I must go hungry, ever again...

To provide food on my table, music on my stereo, books on my bookcase, and games on my forty-inch television?"

"Done done. Is there anything else good sir, before we call this meeting to a close?"

"Yes. I want you to give me friends. Friends, in high places, as well as on the streets.

I want you to give me a family. I want you to give me a degree. I want you to make me a fluid and experienced writer, who people will *want* to read? Not just because they know me!

I want you to take me to conferences in the capital. And make the women who I like to look and stare at, look and stare back at me.

I want you to heal my breathing, the indomitable wheeze, that happens every time I struggle for breath. Stop that.

I want you to make people want to talk to me, rather than just reply out of courtesy. I want you to repair the damage of the social rift, that has happened in my family. Largely my own doing. But I want you to help me heal this, as I indeed am making a conscious choice, to get on better with them myself. To tell me to *stop* when I go too far?!

I want you to make me a
chess grandmaster, so that I can
play players of a much better
rating, say eighteen/nineteen
hundred plus and beat them. I
want you to make me capable to
losing to beginners. Which is a skill
that not many chess *experts*, are
capable of.

I want you to give me
enough money to continue to give
my child pocket money and buy
my family meals to celebrate our
memorable days.

I want you give me a capital
platform, which continues to gain
quarter after quarter. I want you to
reduce my medications, and help
my medical consultant psychiatrist,
to see what it is like to live in my
shoes, as well as do the pre-

emptive risk prevention, on my yearly consultations with him?

I want you to help my wife stay in love with me, and fall in love with me again, if she has fallen out of it?

I want you to improve my acting skills. Characterization, improvisation, and vocalization.

I want you to make me a good person. I want you to heal the wounds of those I have hurt, and rebuild the lives, of those I have destroyed.

I want you to give my nurses and consultants, understanding, and cooperative patients.

I want you to help the cultures and communities I live in, heal, and grow. I want you to bless firstly this world, and dimension, and then the multi-verse and other planets, with love, and understanding and temperance.

I want you to heal the wounds of war and mend the trauma of death.

I want to live, and finally I want to die?"

"We'll see what we can do," the man in the police uniform uniform replied!

27 : Friends

I never really had any friends at school. Sure, I got my first taste of reading, from these studies. And I chatted to some girls in my final year. Even had a girlfriend. But you know, I was kind of a disturbed kid.

Then when I got run over in 1997, gave me a broken neck and serious head injury. Led to a coma, one I have never fully come out of.

I like writing, because here I can return to the world of dreams. In my head and on page, for you our dear readers to share.

Anyway, like I said, I never really had any friends at school. Not at primary school, not at secondary school. Then at college, I made my first friend. A cute girl, who I went later to marry. And she has given me a beautiful stepdaughter.

My sister on the other hand, had loads of friends at primary school, loads at secondary school, and she also met her now husband at university. I used to wonder how she did it.

In the years between me leaving school and getting kicked out from my mum's house at Nineteen, I first made some friends (from my own peer group). And do you want to know how I did it? Well it was by playing online chess, on the computer, on the internet, before the whole 'internet' thing really kicked off...
If I remember correctly, the first two chess applet's (programs), I remember playing were 'Excite' and 'Yahoo' chess. Excite eventually changing hands to 'Pogo' before it became obsolete and disbanded altogether. I remember spending many a glorious hour, on the computer,

trying out various openings, and becoming good at a few of them.

It is a shame really what has happened to online chess nowadays, seeing as computer aided players, although officially refused (like it the server's catch you using an engine to find the 'correct' moves, you *will* be banned), but still people use them. More now than ever before. This explains why we will come across players of pitiful rankings, who will come up with the perfect moves to beat us, time after time. Or almost every time. I know I have already done a chapter on chess, so I won't dwell on this for too long. So, the best we can do to counter this is to adopt 'anti' computer chess tactics. Playing out of the opening book's moves and forcing the struggle of minds to come to the fore. We may come worse off, but at least we will give them a run for their money. Because I tend to find these players who use computer lines, or deeply memorized openings, may flounder and panic when forced into a tactically open middle and end games.

I remember a game I played recently where I kept the enemy on his toes, and then near the end of the game I made an oversight, which left my Queen hanging/exposed, but he didn't see it and retreated instead. Which let me then close in for the win. That felt good.

I do like playing online chess and making friends on here that way. Even if these are people, you will never meet in person, most likely never meet again. It is still a good way to interact. And here on safe spaces on the internet, there is a whole world of geeks, nerds, intellects, and as I said already, cheats, who share the odd half an hour, putting the outside world away, and joining in the battle of sixteen versus sixteen pieces, over a battle terrain of sixty four checked squares. I am very fond of this game. And as I just said, I have made many good friends this way. If you can count digital encounters, as friends?

As for real friends, the flesh and blood variety… It wasn't really until my numerous admissions to hospital from 1997 through to December 2018 (all with psychotic/schizophrenic symptoms), that I changed from a loner without friends, to a popular team player. So, these days, I always have a friend or two I can call on my mobile. And that isn't my dad. Lol.

I feel a bit sorry for our elder generations, who seem to still be struggling to master these new technologies. And compared to our youths, who have grown up with them. It's like the internet.

Yes, I know I have been banned form nearly all the martial arts forums out there, and a good deal more as well. As I have to some extent explored in some of my other books (especially *A Patient in Time*). I mean these days I have been lucky enough to find a small, but decent forum to post in, called (***), who the likes of *** (the owner), and ***, have kept me out of trouble for the past few years. At least I have been able to share some of my life's woes on here, and not be banned.

It is like even at University, I still had a lecturer or three, who seemed to have it in for me. But let's forget about them.

And instead hold on to the great notion of learning and self-improvement, that these institutions hold for us. I must agree, even if I may have struggled to at the time, that these were truly formative years of my life. Not to mention, that my studies kept me out of hospital.

So, friends. Yes study, work hard. But also play hard. Make friends, talk to others. It doesn't matter if you are the most popular person in your class, or one of the loners. Carry on your work. And have faith. Because God loves you. Remember, everyone matures at different rates. And as you do get more mature, and find your niche in this life, so to the dark clouds of our past, will make way for the sunny skies, of our future.

I truly believe in this notion of progress, and hope. And hopefully if you bear with me you can too!

28 : Money

Okay here we go : Money, we all know what that is right? The green you get on pay day, right?

Wrong. I learned a lot of things at my time at university. Not really stuff I was taught, more stuff I picked up myself, along the way. One of which being that money, or wealth, is only what you make of it.

So, what are you most valuable assets? Your house? Your car? Your sky television subscription?

How about your friends, your family, your career, your education?

So, my money? Well for want of betraying confidentiality, it's all these things.

My expertise in surviving the mental health system. Its sure cost me a lot these fifteen years I've been locked away, and on heavy medications. But hell, it must have cost the National Health Service a

comparable fortune, to do this to
me?

Then I think it is in all our
interests, to keep me well, and out
of hospital. And that doesn't
always equate to heavy dose of
medication. Although, it sadly,
seems like it *does*, sometimes…

What else? Back to the realm
of money. Despite not actually
making much, I am sitting on a
healthy trust fund, which protects
my portfolio from the Department
for Work and Pensions, challenges.
It was a hell of a six-month
challenge, to get them to let me
keep this. But I provided the legal
framework/ruling, which in the
end they had to comply with.
And back to my family. I see my
role in this life, now, as that of a
protector. I am here to look after

my wife, and her children. To support them, not just with money, but with *time and love*.

The exact things, I'm not able to provide, from secure hospital settings. So, there you go.

In this life, we don't always have it easy. And whilst faith in God, does help. Sometimes, you need to commit to a hand. And put your chips in investments, that others won't always be able to see, let alone understand.

But trust your own strategies. Make friends. Fight your enemies. Try to avoid breaking the law. But most of all, do what is right.

Whilst God is our ultimate saviour, and judge. So too, we need to live in this life, with the consequences of our actions, and

the knowledge that our legacies
will hopefully be around for a long
time, after our blood and cells,
have returned to the mother Earth,
from whence we came.

And hopefully our spirits
and souls, can return blessed to
their makers.

29 : Gaming Dreams

"So, what did you do today JoJo?"
Today I played on my console. An
Xbox One X.
I played with my daughter. Black
Ops three. Firstly, we played
zombies. And fought off hordes
and hordes of the undead. Firstly,
buying a nice shooting handgun,
then roaming the city, trying to
have the other's back, and wiping

out these undead, until, eventually every time, they became too much for us, and overwhelmed our limited firepower. Especially when our ammo ran out, and we couldn't find the ammo dumps.

"And after that?"

After that I introduced her to a new, bonus, game mode I recently discovered. Free running. There is a total of four courses, and I have completed the first three. The first one, for beginners, is quite nice and simple. A quick jump, or boosted jump, some swimming, fast paddle. The odd target, one of which must be taken on the move, and a couple of wall jumps.

Now these are a little bit tricky at first. And I'll be damned if I haven't got cramp from struggling to master this manoeuvre. It isn't so hard when you only must jump onto a single wall, run along it, and then jump off. Or even from one wall, on to a second.

But when there are multiple walls, then it gets trickier. The real challenge for me today, was something I did before I saw my kid. This was when I tried the third level, which is for experts. And there are a couple of buildings, where starting at the bottom, you must free run up a box structure building with no easy paths. Literally overcoming gravity, and having to build curves into your trajectory, so the right-angle walls, don't stop your momentum. This was tricky. Given the penalties I had to endure for all the restarts I did, I think my record for this level, is something like forty-five minutes. Yes, it really was that hard. And my hand has been in tremor, after all the cramp I have been giving it.

But you know, when, and if I play these free runs again, tomorrow, my hand will be stronger, and better equipped to deal with this brutality.

I realize this may well not seem to relate to martial arts. At least not on appraisal. But don't forget that hand movement and control, is crucial for all the martial arts. At least it is for the four I know best : Kung Fu, Aikido, Judo and Karate. So, the ability to grip, control, project, and counter (reverse), are all hand movements. And with a stronger hand, a more flexible and in control five digits, my martial arts, should, and will, improve alongside.

Not to mention this team playing, with my kid is building a foundation, balancing on the digital world, but aiming at the stars. One day I will be gone. And I can only hope that my daughter is able to share with her children the knowledge and companionship, that we have built together.

30 : Signs of the Zodiac

Control, discipline, friends, family, and love.
We need all these things.
Life is sometimes like a whirlpool, a whirlwind.

Stumbling from step to step, from hold to hold. Out of options, out of gas, out of control.

And where do we end? Where we left off? Or in a different place, a different space. A new galaxy, remedy, or fortune.
If you read the stars, I'm a Pieces. Or by the Chinese zodiac, a Rooster.

I suffer from insomnia. Or maybe sometimes I just forget to go to sleep. My dad blames me for this. But I blame the medications. I have had this problem, right the way through my university life. And boy was I kicking myself when I missed out on a first for my university undergraduate dissertation. But on review, I realized that it had spelling mistakes halfway through the document. And you must appreciate that any spelling mistakes, even one, will prevent this sacrosanct document from ever reaching that pinnacle grade. Which is a shame really. Seeing as I did over a hundred different versions, in preparation.

Later I read that a Bachelor's degree isn't supposed to create *new* knowledge, only better present what's already out there. But I will be damned if I didn't do that and more.

At least I have now paved the way for my daughter and wife, to reach this qualification, if they so choose. A degree, is only as good as the people taking it? Wrong, only as good as the lecturers? To some extent. Maybe only as good as the effort you put in.

Do I regret doing one? Not on your life. I learned so much. About African drama, and education, and sociology, and in my research about mental health. For example, you may have known that during the holocaust, Hitler rounded up the mentally ill, and send them to the extermination camps? But what you probably didn't know is that across Europe, Britain, and even America, there were also programs to Euthanize, sterilize and otherwise deal with the problem patients. The psychiatrists labelled then Dementia Praecox. Now more commonly known as schizophrenia.

So, what else? I did some more gaming today. Reached a couple of new record times for the beginner and advanced Call of duty, Black Ops Three free run courses. This gives me cramp in my left hand, when I play it for too long. Mainly as a result of over pressure on the back of the hand, from having to press down on the left joystick, at the same time as moving to stick, and pressing the buttons with the other hand.

Now the day after, I can play it again, hit the new records, and pull off the moves I was struggling to achieve yesterday, with some ease. I am looking forward to playing on it again with my kid, to impress her with these results. Also, I want to teach her how to wall run up the inside of the buildings, in the penultimate level, which is hard, but there is a trick to it.

What is needed for you to jump at quarter turn angles, with quick succession, to mount the beast. Ride the tiger. If you will excuse my colourful language? Thank God.

Anything else?
No that will do for now. Bear with me. Peace out.

31 : Sharing

When we write, we do so to share with others… It may be a cathartic (healing) process. It may help us to unravel some of the tied-up feelings and tensions, the long day's the past has brought to our shoulders. But all together, it is not only for our eyes to peruse. We write, primarily perhaps, to share these deep harboured secrets with the world.

Some books become best sellers. Others only remain but the domain of the elite few. But the process of writing, and primarily reading (which is, after all, at the heart of every good writer's foundation), is one of sharing. One of therapy. One of memories (*souvenirs* in French). One of times, places, people and moments, locations, facts, and fiction. Writing is, to me, a case of casting the living dynamic world, to a side for one moment. And digging back into that gold mine of your mind, the *good times*. The powerful people we have met, and the memorable moments we have gathered from them.

It is static. It is frozen, forever, on the white paper page of the publication. Whether we have self-published or managed to source a professional to do the job with us.

People, children, our future, our elders and the dead Rest in Peace, the times who have passed before us. And our peers, all battling it out for a slice of the cherry. And does it matter if we win? Does it matter if we become best sellers? What if we discover a new truth in reading? A new sense of competence, a new joy in finding other authors. To share, to explore, to learn from.
There is so much more, to the world, than meets the uniform eye.

And as we learn, we learn that we will always be learning. Or at least, that that is the goal.

One of the beautiful things about doing my Joint Honours Degree, was that rather than just being stuck in the realm of Sociological insight, I also got to learn about Theatrical, (both Shakespeare, and African dramatic) truths. Which at an undergraduate level, is quite impressive? So, for the Shakespeare third year unit, it was standard, for us to be reading a play a week. And then extra backup reading and watching materials as well. It was standard for me to spend many the lunch hour, or late into the afternoons, locked away in the library, head deep in books, or in films. And this was great.

And for the African dramas, discovering new texts, new ways of acting, and researching these, and even finding for example in one of the plays my grandfather Robbie, was mentioned… Everything seemed to be falling in to place. And so, what I only ever got a two : two (C) grade for these modules. In fact I was over the moon to hit these targets, seeing as my class mates were mostly academic young women, many of which had come straight from sixth form education, and were already brimming with the correct academic rigor, to ace these grades. So, like I was saying, up against these star peers, my grades take a new shine.

And so, what if there were at least two (again female) lecturers who clearly had it in for me? Women, who in age terms were my juniors, and gave very little in terms of content, to be taught, in their lectures. And then had the audacity to mark me down, on my essays. Putting ceiling grades of Ds (thirds, or 40%), at the end of these semesters! And you know the way I have learned to research above and beyond the scope of my lesson plans, to find out new ideas and schema, new mod ii, and creations, to adorn my work with. For the presentations, and then bringing these back down to Earth, for classroom, and power-point consumption. Well that went to shoot when I had these time wasters.

It was like, they had lived their whole lives, being at the top of the class, learning their ways. And when somebody stepped out of the folds, and did it a different way, well clearly this was no good for them.

You know the turnover of lecturers across my five-year degree, was quite high. Like a lot. So, to be honest with you, there were only a couple of lecturing staff on my lesson roster, who kept with us from the start. And I've seen at least five, maybe more, lecturers leave, either to better universities (one to Scotland and one to Sheffield), one of my lecturers left to go to Vietnam, to hook up with an old flame, which I don't think lasted, one got the sack because his mathematical statistics, were not taken kindly to by the softer humanitarian approach favoured by my Sociological class mates, and one simply left the undergraduate teaching pool to help out with building the multi-faith centre, although it appears he has now moved on from this as well.

Then this in turn, was then outdone by the number of students who dropped out. I remember one mature student, who was so disgusted by one of the *bad* lecturers, I have already mentioned, that she either felt unable, or was failed by this reader, so that she was *academically* unable, like it was *impossible*, for her to get a passing grade. Which is quite disgusting really? That in this day and age, a university which considers itself to be pretty good, to be employing these people in the first place. This student was a mature student like me, and I remember spending time talking to her, and at that point it was looking doubtful that either of us were going to finish the degree with a pass, let alone honours grade!? I persevered, but I didn't see her on graduation.

Both lecturers I have here mentioned, have stories behind them, which I could ruminate over, but for the sake of anonymity, and to stave of future libel actions, I'm not going to cough up. It is quite disgusting that people like this, who would fail my classmates, because they didn't conform to their mentality, or whatever reason

it was they used to do this. Moving
swiftly on.

Back to the theme at hand :
Sharing. It's something that parents
do with each other when they
make their children. Something
that kids do with their mum and
dads, when they discuss how their
school days had been.

Something that friends do
with each other, when they play
football in the park or the yard, or
play chess or draughts over the
checked board, or cards over the
table.

Actors do on stage, or for
television or the movies.
Something that politicians do with
their peers, their party, their
houses, or representatives,
parliament, the lords, or the senate
Not to mention, and perhaps most

importantly, the public. Both nationally and for the broader global image. They do it to share!?

History is written, and to some extent drafted, by the winners. But it is the people at the bottom, the people sweeping up, the people watching the ten year plus DVD replays, who outnumber these winners by ten thousand to one. And it are these second-rate citizens, our voice, that is just as important as the ruby wielding 'winners' at the top of the spectrum.

They can all go to hell as far as I am concerned!

32 : Bhangra Dancing

Tonight, I danced to Bhangra music, using Kung Fu moves,

which I have creatively Christened Dance Fu! It's something which I used to do quite a lot, at my old address. It lets you try out new moves, whilst developing a good sense of rhythm, and bodily coordination.

I also used two of my favourite Chi Gong moves (similar to Tai Chi, but more closely related to Kung Fu), the first called 'lifting the sky', where standing, you throw your arms out to the side, then lift them up to the top, to connect before bringing them back down in equilibrium, to your centre. And I even extended this to touching my toes a few times (which I barely managed, as I am quite out of shape).

Then the second move is called 'Pushing Mountains', where

you basically lift both hands, parallel to your chest, then extent them outward in front of your, like you are doing press ups in the air. I did these for a song or two as well. These also build internal strength. I didn't do any push ups today. I will save that for another time.

After dancing for seventeen of the songs, I was exhausted. I also did some drunken master monkey dancing, which is basically where you sway from side to side, and throw punches, both closed fist and open handed, as well as giving away the back of your hand, and giving away the palm (which in a real life situation can be converted to a grab, or a throw), and countless Ikkyos, which is the first pin in Aikido. And the only move I can say I am good at. But it's also the first move the police, and security services, use to take down the perpetrators of crime, so it is handy to have in your arsenal.

33 : A Rest in Peace

I remember one of the first times I was arrested, about the turn of the millennium. I had been shown Ikkyo by my auntie's then boyfriend, who was a strong black man called Danny. And he showed me this move. At the time I couldn't remember it, but I have since then been trained in how to do an expert Ikkyo, from firstly Karate classes, then I got it down to a tee with Aikido, which I hold a Yellow belt in.

Danny was a high ranking black belt in Karate, Dan grade material. And whilst after learning this move in two or three demonstrations, in my mum's old front room, I did understand one thing he showed me, which is the first point of this move. Which is to say that that the thumb is the weak point of the grip. For whilst we may have five other non-thumb digits on each hand, we only have one thumb. Consequently, when someone grabs you, it is easier to knock the hand off, using your opposite arm/hand. In a strike to the offending hand, in a forty-five-degree angle to the opposing grip. This releases the grip.

And so, one day, after giving the one finger salute to a police patrol car, then proceeding to being chased away by an irate officer. I didn't get very far before he caught up with me. But imagine the shock on his face, when he grabbed me with his big, manly hand, and I simply knocked it off, with the ease of someone who evidently knew what they were doing. Which seeing as this was the first time, I had used this move, I didn't. But it didn't work, so yes, thanks Danny. Thanks Karate. Ikkyo, which is basically an extension, a fruition, a maturation of this move. Which says, hey, why not rather than just remove his grip, keep it in place, and rotate your body round, again in a forty-five-degree angle oblique to the offender, to bring him down to the ground?

Then some years later, me and Joey, another one of my mentally unstable friends, got in a fight in a city centre cafe. Well I say got in a fight, I attacked him truth be told. But this guy is always such on edge, he really did have it coming to him. Sorry, no, I didn't do Ikkyo, I did another one of my repertoires of killer martial arts moves. The "headlock", which brought him crashing down over the tables and patrons, all of whom tried to look away, as I punished him. Okay, this is graphic language, and Joey was, and always will be a mate. But he did tell me that it messed him up for a good while afterward. Anyway, we made up.

And you know even the headlock, which is a powerful move, when used correctly, has a development, maturation, which goes from nasty, to killer. Which is reverse Guillotine. Which is effective on the floor in groundwork, Judo randori for example. But a killer when used on the street, on an unsuspecting perpetrator.

Which is exactly what I did do, a while after the scrap with Joey. Some homeless punk once saw me walking to my local gym, which is in the city centre, and saw my large purse, protruding from my jacket, nabbed it, and ran away from me (legged it). Well not wanting my martial art's training to fail me, I chased him up the street, and put him down using this very move. The reverse Guillotine. He was so shocked at this move, plus it attacks the spine near the base of the neck, so caused a temporary black out. In this time, I retrieved my Chinese medicine balls, which he had also nabbed, but forgot to pick up my purse/wallet. So, then I waited for a bit, in which time, he revived, saw that my purse was still there for the plucking, picked it up and ran off. I was later able to reclaim the money taken out from my wireless credit cards, because they are insured. So, this is the second move I was able to use effectively on an unsuspecting opponent.

34 : Other ideas

Do I know any other martial arts moves? A few. Break-falling, which I learned at Judo as a kid, and then again at Aikido. Whilst the break-fall necessarily interrupts the collision of your body, when after being thrown/taken down, with the slap of your arm/hand. Because it is better to let a limb take the shock of this collision, than suffering the damage to the torso/midriff/centre.

I'm not going to slag off my martial arts teachers. Because we need to respect our elders. But I have my own way, and my own learnings, which much like doing the degree, are something, a way if you will, which I have now honed, and refined. And cannot be taken away from me, just because they don't mar with their learned ways. Please read my second and third books, A *Patient in Time : JoJutsu* and *Fighting Madness* both available at Amazon and all good bookstores, if you want further insight into the genesis, engagement, development, and fruition of my martial art. In that book I called it JoJutsu, not to be confused with the staff fighting discipline which shares the same name. But instead, an ontology rooted in the central character of many of my stories. Jo. Or as in here, to use his full name JoJo. `Good luck`!

35 : Life's Challenges

In this life we are faced with challenges. From emerging from the womb, to learning to crawl, walk, speak, and read.

We struggle through school, college, and university. Struggle to hold down a job. Keep hold of a loved one. And then watch as your child goes through the same traumas we did.

Only we hope that their lives are easier than ours were. We want them to climb and soar, where we stumbled and fell.

So is it easy? Sometimes. Sometimes it is incredibly hard. There is a wide range of literature available today, from both online stores (notably Amazon and eBay), the brick and mortar bookshops (Waterstones springs to mind), and now in the digital age even Kindle and Google books, vie for position in this ever evolving world.

But whilst some people may like to sit down with an eBook, I much prefer a paper, or hard back edition. I say we must prepare our children for the world, to give

them opportunities so they don't
suffer like we did. But the sharpest
swords, are forged in the hottest
fires. And we can't molly coddle
our children for all their lives in
case they never grow up.

It's like me learning how to
cook. I first learned in home
economics lessons, at secondary
school. Which were good. These
helped. That is where I first
learned to make my legendary rock
buns.

But over the years, especially
living by myself, I have picked up
some good skills such, as gaging
how hot an oven, or plate, is
needed, before putting the food
in/on.

Some people have only ever
cooked by the book. So, if you ask
them to cook a staple food, pasta

for example, without a timer, they will struggle.

Or like being a vegetarian. It was always a lifelong dream of mine, to stop eating meat once and for all. Which seems to be a target I have been doing quite well at sticking to, for the past couple of years or so.

When I was in hospital, I sometimes ate meat. I mean there is such a limited range on the menu, it was out of sheer desperation if anything. A cry for help.
But would I recommend their meat? No sorry. With pork, beef, and fish, that don't reassemble anything known to man. Perhaps I am being mean. But the meat wasn't great!

36 : A letter to the powers that be

I'm kind of like a prisoner of war. In two thousand and three I opposed the invasion of Iraq, and subsequent capture and execution of Saddam, I have been arrested and sectioned, more times since, than beggar's belief. I distinctly remember being kept in the ward at the Kingsway intensive care unit PQ, with an air-light, for the burning summer of 2007. That was difficult. We nearly cooked alive!

Also, all my crimes, up to two thousand and seventeen were, (except for me smashing up the Ford Escort car in 2005), were committed on a ward, when I was on medication. I know you have a responsibility to the public, to keep them safe from me. And I have tried to work closely with my social care team, mum, dad, sister, wife, consultant, and community treatment manager.

This road has taken a long time. And I'm thirty-nine now, so I'm not getting any younger. My wife has been a godsend and blessing, and she continues to meet me. I want to stay well so that I can continue to see them. Even my last doctor agrees how much better I am on this new medication.

I don't know what your criteria are for me coming off them, or at least having the medications reduced are? Hopefully you can see for yourself the progress I have made. I have also switched from cigarettes to vaping about six months ago. Today my dad suggested waiting two years, before any reduction takes place. And if you are happy with this, I am prepared to concur. Up to you? J

37 : Respite

Sleep. That most beautiful of things, when you lay down on your pillow, and let the world of troubles wash over your head. You close your eyes and return to the land of dreams. Where the troubles of your life, wash away. And the angels of your life, return to the playing field.

I suffer from insomnia. That is where, I struggle to sleep at a decent time. Often find me awake for twenty-four, thirty-six, or even longer periods of time. I find myself reassembling a vampire, zombie, or werewolf in that respect.

Sometimes, I log in to my games at night. Be it Call of Duty, Lichess, or Dominance Poker. Sometimes I do cook, sometimes (quite frequently) listening to music. A range of activities, to keep myself occupied at night.

I once imagined myself to be an old general. Navigating the battlefields, on my horse, like Napoleon, or Wellington. And commanding my armies, to fight off the hordes of trolls, zombies, and demons, that would affront us daily. And there were times when I was knocked off my horse, and again like Napoleon, taken captive on an island, to serve my time. This is how I felt, every time I was captured, by the mental health services. A prisoner, a prisoner of war.

And rather than just comply, I would fight them. From expressing my individuality, and with kisses, to asking them not to give me the iron tablets, or antibiotics. Which always seemed to mess with my internal constitution.

I don't like taking drugs. And fair play to them, they know as well as I do, that I am hoping for the day, when I can come off them all together.

I have been on anti-psychotic medications, of one sort or another, for the best part of fifteen years.

Over which course, I have had over a dozen hospital admissions, in and out, generally lasting Seven months. But the last time I went in, it was for two years. Both here in Derby, and over to Bradford, for a sixth month stint. Boy that was a killer. Imagine going from a thirty a day smoking habit, to none. This was tough. And for all these prisons and hospitals, which have banned smoking completely, fair play to them. God knows how they do it.

Then I would get two a day, then four, finally six, eight, and I think eventually I was let back home to Derby.

I met Michael Jackson in hospital. Or at least I thought it was him? It may not have been, but he did a Jackson style twirl, and I have never known anyone else who could do this? He told me how upset he had been when the social services took his kids off him. That is further evidence. And he taught me the importance of knees and elbows, in a street fight! This was good practical advice, which may one day save my life?! He got out before me; I hope he is okay.

I also met a guy who I called Vietnam child. He reminded me a son I might have had with Min, my Chinese 'friend', I met at a charity shop some years earlier. I never slept with her, only cuddled her on a couple/few occasions. And I'm not sure if you can make a baby, that way. Anyway …

So yes, I was able to connect Vietnam kid, with his family, on the pay phone. Who were eventually able to visit, and then rescue him, from this trap?

I also met an atheist friend, from Afghanistan, I think. He didn't really speak much English, if any. But I was able to communicate with him, by a combination of sign and body language. I also thought he was blind, by the way he seemed to stare. I even on a couple of occasions, closed my eyes, and tried to navigate the small area which consisted of the ward, by touch and memory alone. This was difficult, but gives me some good insight into the perils, and hardship, blind people face. The things we do when we are mad!

And finally, there were a
good number of admirable staff
members here. Probably the most
famous one, was Alex Ferguson,
who had retired from football, to
become a senior carer, at this
mental health unit. He was a good
guy. And I was sad to find out he
died, a few years later. At least that
was what I heard?

There were also a couple of
staff members who I don't think
they were an item, although they
might have been. Anyway, they
had both served as royal officers, in
the armed or naval services. And I
was impressed by their courage,
and steadfast determination, to
look after their wards, and help us
all get better.

There were a lot of other people on this unit as well. Hell, I have met a lot of people over the years, some of my best friends, have been made in hospital. And I have known a lot of good staff workers as well. I tip my hat to them I really do.

Okay boys and girls, I think that is about enough on this topic, of sleep, and hospital. I hope I will never have to go in again, but statistically I would say the odds are against me. At least now, I have a stable home life, with regular visits from my family, and a close connection to my carers, as well as other friends, I talk to, and see on a regular basis. Take good care, and sweet dreams.

38 : Health

Control. Respect. Love.
Remember the good times. Think
about them. Remember the friends
you have made along the way, new
ones too. Focus on them.
People you have met,
conversations you have had. Places
you have been to. Good music, that
you have listened to.

  This life isn't a short one. You
have lived for a long time, and God
willing you have a long time to go.
Don't rush into things. But if you
do, embrace them. Hold on to
what's good. Read, play, eat, sleep.
I wish I could sleep. It's like back in
'97 I went into a coma, one which
I've still not fully woken up from.

Glimpse your medical infirmities and try your best *despite* these.

Spend your money wisely, when you have it. And when you don't, save.

How many times do I have to say this to you? You are beautiful. And it doesn't matter who you are, or what you are feeling right now. Every man and woman, who has ever loved, was once a baby. The greatest pinnacle of humanity. Remember this. Hold on to this hope. And no matter your position, whether you consider your life a success, or a failure at this point. There is still time to turn it around.

Take it from me, the man who once hit rock bottom. From a Primary and Secondary education. To get hit by a speeding car and face my first seven-month hospital

admission. From losing my first and only true friend, when she left the country, and I thought I might never see her again. To being kicked out of my house and sleeping rough for a night.
The car accident, eventually some years later, won me a decent playout. But for over ten years after this, the money was locked away. And these so-called expert solicitors, did a damn fine job at spending it for me. Until there came the point, when it looked as if my money wouldn't even last me another five years, let alone the rest of my life.

And then there was my mental health problems. Something one of my consultant psychiatrist's, flattering called, *acute* and *chronic* Schizophrenia. Charming.

I have also been told by several medical professionals, that this is a lifelong condition, which I will have to take medication for, for the rest of my life? Am I happy with this? You better not believe it.

It is my good intentions to prove them all wrong!

You see I am on something called a community treatment order now, which is a section, they place on the most ill in the community. And at every review I have, which must be carried out by a doctor, a social worker, and a lay person, I think... Well I always present my best self, for coming off it. But at every review, at every tribunal I've ever had, they always reach the same decision. That it is better for me to stay on the C.T.O., rather than come off it. This is to starve off the risk of noncompliance with medicine, and medical treatment. Bull basically.

So, what else? My dad thinks he knows me. He thinks he has read my books, and supported me through it? But was he there when I got hit by a car? Was he there when they attached electrodes to my skull, and administered high voltage electric currents? Was he they when I asked my solicitors, before the case was settled, to accept a lower award, because I was just frustrated at how long the whole thing was taking, and wanted to be done with it?

Was he there, when my wife won
the visa, in Nottingham
magistrates court (a big glass
building in Nottingham, near the
train station)? Was he there when I
had to settle the barrister's fee,
which came to many thousands?
Was he there, every time I got
admitted? Was he on the ward
with me, for every ward round,
when I argued my silly socks off
with the doctors, only to be told
time and time again, that they *still*
thought I was ill, and treatment?
Time and time again!
Was he there when I got taken out
of the court of protection?

I haven't been able to hold
down a job for most of my working
life, and all bar a few charity jobs
and one brief stint at a nursing
home, none. Be the crimes that I

have committed will stay on my record. I seriously struggle at seeing me *ever* holding down, a nine to five job. It's okay…

I have been blessed to have met these two wonderful people. And every hour, every minute, every second I spend with them, being from the visits I get, or the telephone contact, well this is all when I am touched by heaven.

I will be sad when we must leave each other, as death separates, us all from our loved ones, in the end. But I am hoping to still have many more special moments, and times, before that day comes. But by then regret will be too late. Let's hope that I can make up for the bad karma I had as a youth, with some positive energy I have been able to kindle as a man.

39 : Recovery

Let us move on. I have magical powers. Ask any of my friends, and they will be able to confirm this for you. The doctor says I don't have insight. But that is not true. I did a five-year degree, where every day I had to come to terms with my illness, to get the job done. And I only missed like one or two days over the whole five years, which was due to seasonal viruses. Where it would have jeopardized the safety of others, for me to go in. Anyway, back to the magic. Today, I turned the heating off in my lounge, and put it on in my bedroom, then went outside for a vape (I have stopped vaping in the house).

I have lived in my own house since the break of the year. Cooked my own food (cheesy pasta with mayonnaise and sauce), washed my own dishes, paid my own bills, and washed my own clothes. At the break of the year, I was also successful in winning my benefits, both full Universal Credit, and full Personal Independence payments. My once sweetheart left the country half the way though our college education, and never returned. At least that was how it seemed.

I finally managed to get her phone number, and hold the odd conversation with her, and write and receive the odd latter. But Still the future was looking bleak. Then finally in 2007 I was able to fly over to visit her. And she begun to make a man out of me. In 2008 we got married.

In 2012 I was able to visit again. This time doctor Tao told me the two conditions of me going, was that I took an injection dose over, to be administered over there. And that I took the anti-malaria tablets. Ever though I had had a severe reaction to them, the first time I took them. I took them prior to flying, and on the plane, but in Kenya I was so sick from a reaction to these tablets, that we agreed I wouldn't need to take them anymore.

This whole idea of me having no insight in to Schizophrenia is nonsense. I spent the whole of my final year at university studying it.

From the black person's experience on locked wards, to the Nazi's final solution, and other varied, and complex ideas (see appendix). The final chapter in my essay, was on insight. And I have printed this off for you know. How the hell could I write a high-level piece of academic literature, on this subject, and not have at least a basic insight into the condition. It wouldn't be possible.

My community nurse and consultant have been using the same tripe lines "oh he's a risk to himself and others", "oh he would come of his medications if taken off a C.T.O.". Tell me then, why for the seven years I was at university I persisted in taking them, even though halfway through when I was taken off the order (by mistake) I still took them at full dose?

I know you guys are so enamoured by these overpaid medics, I have had loads of tribunals before, and lost everyone. And it is always the same old arguments. Basically, it is me the little guy in the bottom, who must take it in the neck.

I'm not trying to deceive you. Unlike the *Doctors*, who change their stories every time, like a chameleon. I try to always tell the truth. Why the hell would I confess my sins, what possible good does that do me? Do you really think I just needed to get it off my chest? Idiots. No, I will tell you why I mentioned her, because I'm not afraid to tell the truth.

And the whole issue of magic, is kind of hard to explain. But my magical powers do increase, with the reduction of these medications. Sure, I want to come off them one day. But that day isn't today.

What I want today, is for you to remove this legal shackles, from around my neck, and also get an assurance from doctor Tao, or his successor, that they will agree to reduce my dose from the 405 mg it is at the moment (the maximum dose), to the 300 mg dose, which is the next step down.

I visit my nurse for the injection every month, without fail. This will continue. She has even offered to do extra meetings (to monitor my progress) if I do have this reduction. So, it's not as if there isn't a strong framework in place, to detect any sign of a relapse. I also have weekly visits by the community psychiatric nurse, and twice or thrice weekly visits by my support worker from Rethink.

Get off my back. Grow up, grow some, and leave me alone!

PS. Sorry for getting angry, but how would you feel if you had to spend the next fifteen years of your life, in and out of hospital, and under huge amounts of pressure over this time. That is the reason I want the C.T.O. removing, to treat me like a human being, and not some subhuman, who can maintain a marriage, and home, and stepdaughter, and not be trusted to take my medication?

40 : Fight

Tonight, I got in a fight. Randori, sparring, call it what you want, with Will. It was the first one we have had in a while. And the same as the previous two, it ended in a draw.

It lasted two rounds. But whereas the first one saw me gassing out early, in this one I still gasses out in the first round, but I lasted the two, before we both agreed to call it quits. A draw.

But whilst I gassed out, he showed me his hands and he was shaking all over. I call that a psychological victory. And we could have gone on further, but like I said I didn't want to hurt him. I guess I need to start doing some more pushups, to build my anaerobic strength, and more long-distance walks, to build my cardiovascular strength.

There was a point when I saw an opening for a kick, so I threw a quick right front kick at his leg. Only lightly, because as I said I didn't want to hurt him. And then he changed his guard to watch out for my legs. We both went in with some punches, and he is lucky that I took my surrogate wedding ring off, because my left jab would have dominated him. I went to grab him a few times, and he didn't try any single arm grabs, but we did stand still for a minute or so, just holding on to each other.

I tried to apply pressure to make him fall to the ground, but he has good balance, and was able to resist this.

Then I got the front kick in, I already mentioned. I also saw an opening for a head butt, which would have done some serious damage to his face I'm sure. But like I have said, I didn't want to hurt him. Plus, I can save this move for the future, depending on what else happens.

I have also yet to use my trademark headlock, or reverse guillotine on him, which I have ended two separate fights within the past, with equal success. One against my mate Joey, who later told me I had him by surprise, and the other against a mugger in town, whom I was able to retrieve at least half of the booty he had stolen that day.

We even had a friend act as referee, and simultaneously film the fight on her phone. At least she said she filmed it. She also said that she would be uploading the video to Facebook, that night I thought. But she hasn't so far. Which makes me think that perhaps she didn't even film it in the first place. No matter. Another result for the angels. And the clouds where they live.

I think for the next fight, I am going to ask her to film it using my phone's video camera, so at least that way I will know that it has been recorded. And whilst it is true that the car park we squared off in, it was like midnight. So, all the neighbours were in bed. At least no one disturbed us. And like I said, we did have a ref.

But me and Will are good friends. He even said that he was just going to block my punches, although when the fight got started, we both got in some *Atemi* (strikes).

It's been over four years since I last did Aikido, and seven since I did it with a club that teaches the 'hard' way, so you might say I am a bit rusty. But I have been doing some, if albeit small martial arts practice by myself, and even one session with my daughter and other friends, so I'm not completely useless. Like I said, I am going to start to be less sedentary, and more proactive. Walking to town for example, more often at least. Public transport surely is a blessing when the buses decide to arrive on time that is, at least. But walking, one step in front of another, is truly a treasure, and one which I have been neglecting of late. I need to get more into it. Plus, I want to do some more press ups. Hell, I will do some now. Give me a minute, and let me see how many I can do...

There you go. Fifteen. Not bad. I once did Fifty. If I do them every day, I should hit this target soon. But it does gas me out. We will see.

I'm pleased that me and Will are sparring again. I have been sorely missing this aspect of live combat, and assuming I don't get any threats by my landlord, then hopefully we can continue this pattern.

I am considering asking him to start on the floor, so we can practice our groundwork. Something we haven't been doing, as of late. With no strikes or kicks allowed. Or at least from the standing clinch. Again, with no strikes. Just the clinch, throws/takedowns, and on the ground, from the mount, to half guard for example/

I am confident if I put him in *Kesa-Gatame* (the Scarf Hold, which is the first judo hold you will learn, well it's the first I was taught anyway), he would struggle. Well today he told me that he did Judo and Wrestling at school. Which is a possibility. Because like I said, today he fended off my attacks well, leading to the draw. But you know, it could also be lies, god knows.

At least if we start on the ground, there will be no testing of our break-fall apparatus, and it can be dangerous falling on sheer concrete. And instead the two of us will have to rely on touch, and the great Mixed Martial Art videos we have watched, to give us inspiration for the moves to pull. Which should be funny, seeing as I don't think either of us have watched that many! Laughing out loud.

Oh well. He's going on holiday tomorrow, for a couple of weeks, so that will give me, and both of us, a chance to heal and get our act together for the next bout. Should be fun, and hopefully I will be able to get it recorded next time, as well.

41 : The Blues

I thought I had lost you. I thought I would never see you again. I thought that the time we had spent together, were over. The joy I had shared in our presence was no more. That my life was over.

The music which I'd spent the years hoping for, dreaming for, were no more.

I was close to giving up. To seeking solace elsewhere.

But then I picked up the guitar. Played a chord. Played another. Kept the hope alive in my heart, whereas elsewhere it was dead.

Kept the Blues alive, on this guitar, in this house, at this juke box.

And slowly, oh so slowly, we were able to revive the bird from the ashes. The legendary Phoenix, everyone else had long given for dead, who had closed her eyes and said he final prayer, was once again, able to rise from the ashes, and like our heavenly father, return to the Earth once more.

This simple song, with simple notes, simple chords : Brings back to life, the faith. The faith of the dead and dying, and now the faith of the children. And the men and women.

This life we lead is often a simple one. And at times it is complicated, oh so heavy. Then we move it forwards and bring it closer to our heart. With a jukebox and a stereo. Or a television and a games console. A subscription, and an hour to enjoy it.

Some quality time with our loved ones, and a prayer for the dead.

And slowly, carefully, we can nurture the love we thought was dead. Spend time with her. When we can. And keep a space next to our heart, so that when we can't be together, the space is taken.

Hasn't this always been the way of man? To lament the gone, and treasure those that are still here?

For the kings and the princes, and for the queens and the princesses? They all share the stage with us.

A single life is all we are given. Please make the most of it. I should say I will see you in the next one, but it will be too late then. We shouldn't count our blessings. But make the most of this one. You only live once. And for the future? What doors will be open for us? For our children, and their children? For the rest of mankind?

Will they finally be able to close the doors to suffering and hardship, and give way to a future of hope and resilience? So, they don't have to suffer like we did? Like our parents did? And their parents?

Can the fiction of the past be finally put to bed, and make way for a future of hope and truth? Of companionship and brotherhood? Wasn't this the dream of our elders, from the French American and Portuguese revolutions?

Don't give up your dreams. I brought them here to live with me. But I couldn't hack it. Now I must work every day to keep hold of them. And when I die, I can kiss the world goodbye. I'd like to think that my life can act as a beacon for others who have suffered in the mental health system. And I am worried that the mistakes I have made, will leave a stain on my memory.

Honestly, if you have got with me this far, got with us this far, then you have done well. So, some parting words? Avoid the beer and wine, it will be the death of you. And avoid the cigarettes as well because they are also no good. Keep on doing what you are good at. If you can find someone to love,

hold on to them. Never let her/him
go.

42 : Music

I find that playing the steel strung
Spanish Acoustic Guitar, to be a
little rough on my hands. So, for
example the left hand must hold
down the strings on the notes, and
the right hand must pluck them.
Or if you are so lucky as to own a
pic, then you can strum, or pic
them, using this device. In fact,
today I purchased some pics, as
well as a Blues guitar book, and I
am feeling quite optimistic in my
music playing. Like I can push the
boat, further out in my practice
sessions. Get further along with the
practices. And learn more.

Plus, today I had my hair cut, and one of the neighbouring hairdressers commented on how much better my breathing is, then as to the old times I used to see him. I think this is true. And like I told him, I consider the fact that we seem to be on a better medication now, is a large part of why this is good. I think the meds suit me, and the fact that I am in a good place with regards to my housing and family life, all contribute to my positive health outlook.

I don't know if I told you this, but a few days ago I levelled up on Call of Duty Black Ops Three, then a private, now a middle Sergeant. Which was because I was able to get some kills in. You see in this game, on online mode, you only level up if you kill the other players. Not in real life, but on the game. And using my Kudo fully automatic machine gun, you only must line them up with the sites, and hold the right trigger down for a moment, and they are blown away.

The thing is, when I first owned this game, like a few years ago, and I played in online then, I was truly useless. And couldn't get kills in if it was the end of me. But since then I have completed the first and second Black Ops games and got better at this the third one. So for example I have progressed far enough to unlock the safe-house, and also the computer terminal and internet, which has told me about smart technology, smart materials for example, able to use camouflage as a part of the soldier's uniform. To make them blend in with the scenery. Quite exceptional.

So anyway, I was playing the game, running in to hailstorms of bullets, and catching a foe or three on the way.

Then something quite remarkable started to happen. We were playing team games, where the victor is decided by the kills, and possession of the node/orb, and I was being assigned a minder. Basically, a guardian who hold back with me, at the back, near the base, deep into our held territory, and then he or she who take care of any enemies who approached and tried to scalp me. And when that happened, I even tried to scarper, to hide, and run from the bullets. This tactic seemed to work quite well, and I think as a team, we won at least two best of three games, in this way.

The games are a team effort, and by uniting, it really felt like we were achieving something greater. Hell, I can't wait to show this new game mode to my daughter, whom I'm sure will take to it like a duck to water. I will explain to her, that if she is worried, she can just hold back, and return to safety. Hopefully she will get a guardian, in the same way I did. Nice game.

So why was I talking about this? Because believe it or not, playing Call of Duty has a connection to playing the guitar, in that they both take good hand strength, as well as good eye to hand coordination. And despite not having played much of the guitar in these last three years or so, I have been plugging away at my games. Not just Call of Duty, but also Fallout 4, which was another challenge with regards to eye to hand coordination, and hand strength. As well as the Tekken's before that.

You probably think that I'm beating around the bush. Well if you want me to talk about the recent disaster which has been my internet train wreck of recent days, I will get to that. But I must be careful over what I say. So not as to further offend anyone, and so I can try to set the record straight, with regards to my position in the field. Once and for all.

43 :

Where do we come from? Where are we
going when we die?
Who gives us our freedoms? Who brings us
together?

God is all these things. His love
provides for us, in the cold, in the dark,
after bereavement. He does not judge. He
does not blame. He provides us a light in
the darkness. Hope when it is all done.

We need God. He has lots of
different names. God, Jesus, Jehovah,
Mother Nature, Sophia, and Allah. We need
love. He is our friendships. He is our
health. He is our love.

Without God we have nothing. And
alone in a barren universe, we are but
atoms which bounce into one another.
Terminal, finite, limited, closed, and
stopped. With God we have harmony, we
have union, we have hope, we have wealth
we have a future.

God is in all of us. From the moment
you take your first breath, to when you sigh
your last. He is there. He was there for you,
and he will stay there till the end. He knew

you before you were born, and he will stay with you when you die. Right by your side.

Believe it or not my books are a chance for me to pay homage to him. To spend time with the written word, to seek out the truth, to find allies in my readers, and negate the dark forces of Satan in advance.

Please stay with me. And if you have got this far, you certainly have done. Sometimes we forget to honour our parents. Our grandparents and our heavenly father. We continue through live as driving on autopilot. Not bothered by the other road or pavement users. We need to take heed. And consider that our every action, and every reaction, has already been written. God gave us freewill. Which enables us to take hold of our lives and craft a destiny. He also gave us companionship, and family, which gives us goals and friendships and hope. He loves us.

As a child I was without God. I went to a secular school and came from a heritage of strict Atheism. It wasn't until after I have spent many months in hospital, that I discovered the hospital chapel. And the hope I found in prayer there, as well as songs of praise, opened a new spiritual dimension to my life, I never knew was possible.

I don't like these street preachers, who shut down their verses, down our ears, as if their faith is the only one. Each person has their own conviction and truth. Each person, man woman and even children, are free to build their own connection with our creators. We may not like it; we may not be able to look him in the eyes but remember that we are remembered. That we are praised, and we are loved. And just as every mother loves the new-born babes, so too God loves us.

Industry, and work are admirable qualities if you can produce them. All our companionships, unions, hopes, are listened to. God will and does provide justice for all our misdemeanours. And just as Tony Blair, must pay with his conscience for the million innocent civilians he killed in Iraq, and you can see he is a broken man, haunted by this fact. So too we all must pay for our crime.

I nearly lost my wife and kid. I am still holding on to them but find it hard to do so. My god provides me with contact with them, and gives me a future, whereas the annihilation of a strictly non forgiving justice system, would have long thrown away the key to my jail cell. I'm lucky they didn't charge me.

I like to think that it is because of the strength of my relationship with the girls, that the years I have supported them, both here in the United Kingdom, and when they were over in Africa, stood for something. That the strength of the foundations we have built in our lives, mean something, and that it is not just them, but our forefathers and mothers in heaven, who can speak up for me in the eternal judgment.

Yet I know that our support workers, and justices, also will have exercised caution, both in their decision to separate them from me, for their safety, as well as that of others. And, to give me a lifeline and future, in giving me contact with them here forth.

I am also very aware that I am on my final warning. Perhaps I have passed it? And as every good yarn needs a strong beginning, closure is also needed. So, am I ready to give up on them? Not yet. I am still trying.

44 :

BANG

The lights went out. Slowly I came to. But I couldn't move. My body was fixed. Tied to a bed. I could hear, just about. I remember my mother sitting by my side. Every day. In hospital. In Intensive care.

I was in a coma. All my fears, true. Realized. All my hopes, my ambitions, my dreams, dropped.

There was nothing. Only darkness. I had a tube up my throat and down my soldier.

I couldn't breathe. I couldn't wee. I couldn't speak.

They did a life test on me. I got a three. We thought that was close to death. Negative.

Three is the lowest on the scale I found out later. I was in effect, dead.

And so how did I come back? Mainly through the love of my mum. The woman who suckled me and stood by my side through the hell of years I endured at school. Where I only survived through nightly excursions on my personal computer. Playing games.

But here I was at life's edge. And fighting for my life. This was a difficult period for me. And the day our good princess died, was the day I walked again. Never mind.

I made it. Someone who thinks they have done something, don't know the meaning of trial, until they have faced coma.

So, when I was there on that bed, do I remember what happened to me. After twenty-three years? The day I died, but my parents didn't turn off the machines. I was given another chance at life. The chance to turn my life around.

To fall in love. To become a parent. To write books. What's up with that?

And they complain when I haven't been able to hold down jobs? When I am not very good at keeping my flat tidy.

That I struggle to maintain a good sex drive.

So, I surround myself with people that love me. With people that have experienced a single per cent of the pain I have suffered. And I have recovered. Slowly

The coma stays with me. I get cold hands, even a cold bum. I am on such a high dose of medication, that they must keep me on the ward for three hours after each jab. And it is a mean big old needle that goes in my bum.

But I am out of that now. I am a survivor. I have the love of a good woman and her child, something that many others will never have, and I am grateful.

I must temper my actions. Remember the good will and prayers, that kept me alive in my darkest hour. Not to mention the sacrifices given to me by my mum, dad, and sister, for every friend who came to visit me in hospital, and every neighbour that said a prayer when I was that close to death. God bless them.

45 : Daisy the Cat i

Daisy was a cat. She was a very special cat. She was rescued as a young cat, from a house where they had a lot of cats. And the owners didn't treat them very well. Daisy had lots of brothers and sisters and was always fighting with them for food. Plus, the owners treated them as animals, not giving them individual love. And so, in this way, the early formative years of her life were quite cruel and harsh.

One day the owners decided to get rid of her. And she was lucky, that her new owners, JoJo, and family, agreed to take her in. But after being transported to her new address, she was scared. In fact, she was terrified. So, for this reason, the minute she was taken out of the cat box from the car journey (and like most other cats, she *hated* being in that box in the car), she immediately ran to safety. Hiding away in the corners of the living room. Behind the sofas, deep into the corners of the room. And no amount of gentle "here kitty kitty", would coax her out of this abyss.

JoJo and his daughter used to leave food for her on plates. And little by little, steady by steady, the food would go missing. At night, the plate would have cat food on it, either the biscuits, or as she preferred the jelly, and in the morning the food wouldn't be there. At first daughter thought there had been a thief in the house.

How dare they enter the premise and steal this poor kitten din dins. But how could this be? They always locked the doors and checked the windows were secure. So how could this be happening. But then, slowly over the coming days, Daisy would start to show her face. She became stronger, and more confident as the days rolled into weeks. Showing more and more of her black and white fur. Gaining new confidence in JoJo and daughter. So that eventually she would even come out from hiding, and eat, and even watch tv with the owners.

They say cats have nine lives. I think Daisy has had some of hers, given what I put her through! But even today, Daisy is still a much-loved cat. With a strength, only distinctive to her mum and aunty.

She would catch mice, and the odd bird. In fact, she used to like it when JoJo trailed a string, in front of her. So, she could catch that, it's a feline reflex, to catch the mice. And together with her new owners, she used to spend many happy days, chasing these imaginary mice.

Once she caught fleas. And this was a problem. The local supermarket sold special cat de-flea potion, which you had to rub a little bit behind her ears, and it was supposed to deal with this problem. Well they did that, and it did after a few days, clear the problem. But by that time the house was pretty much infested with fleas. And only repeated cleaning, hovering, and wiping the surfaces down, would eventually deal with this problem. In fact, Daisy was cured of the fleas, a long time before they had left the house altogether.

Cats are different from dogs. Whereas a dog is loyal and a companion, cats are more independent. I'm not saying you can't make friends with cats. God help us, are well looked after cat is a good friend, much in the way a well-fed dog can be. But it takes time. And if you compare the noises they make, a dog barks, which is like a little more aggressive, to a cat's meow. Which is more subtle. But they are clever, and they can understand quite a lot of human speech. If not at first, they pick this up over time.

Daisy was a good cat. And as I have said already, she was a special cat. She needed this inner strength and fortitude, to survive the challenge, which was to occur a few years on. When she was locked in the house, without food or water, for a matter of three weeks (or more). But whereas any other pet, would have died from this trauma, Daisy survived. She wasn't happy. She did nearly die. And when after those three/four weeks the front door finally opened, she shot out faster than a bullet on speed. And JoJo would never see her again.

But she returned eventually to my daughter, and finally settled in their new home. Which was another home, another flat. A brand-new start.

JoJo was sorry that he had left her alone in this way. At the time he wasn't right in his head. He had been going through a very difficult period. And this had terminated in his apprehension and detention by the powers that be, followed by a police arrest, a period of sleeping rough on the street, and a violent knockout blow. As well as having thrown the keys he had for that old flat, down the drain. So that even if had wanted to save Daisy, this was out of his hands.

He was transferred from the police holding cell, to a secure locked psychiatric ward (again), and Daisy was alone. No more imaginary cats to play with, no tastier cat food, or cooling water to drink. She was left to die. She thought the whole world had forgotten about her. And as the hours rolled into days, and the days in two weeks, she had almost given up hope. But then returned to her. She was fed and watered, and eventually brought back to health.

But she vowed she would never forgive me for this, what he had done to her. Even though, he didn't consider himself fully responsible for this animal cruelty, in that it was first the police, and then after the hospital, which had detained him, and prevented him from saving Daisy, she was still his ward, and his responsibility.

And it wasn't just Daisy, but the cats of the world, which took this blow. But as I said already, she grew stronger, and back to health eventually. And even if JoJo did never get to meet her again in person, she was able to show him photos of her progress, and so he still loved her, even if this was only one way.

46 : Daisy the Cat ii

The next day was grim outside. It was dark, and it was cold. JoJo felt tired. He wasn't sure how long he had been sitting in the chair for, much less how much longer he would be there. He felt tired, and thirsty.

A moment later the door opened, and two uniformed officers entered.

"JoJo, are you okay?"

"I'm fine".

"Would you like a glass of water?"

He hesitated, and then shrugged his shoulders.

"Sure"

The sound of a toilet flushing, and a beat later one of the officers re-entered holding a white Styrofoam cup.

"Here you go…"

"Thanks" JoJo mumbled, took the fine beverage, and downed the lotion in one.

"Now what do you want to ask me today?"

"JoJo" the officer continued, "remember you are here of your own free will. At any point you can choose to end the interview and walk out of our office. You haven't been charged, and you are still a free man!"

"So If I choose to walk out now, I'd get as far as the exit… you wouldn't arrest me then, you wouldn't rugby tackle me to the ground, and give me an acuphase depot injection, to make me fall asleep until the next day?"

"No, we wouldn't".

"You're a liar officer. I know this game, as much as anyone, I know the consequences of acting deviant to the norm. Of thinking outside of the box. Of breaking the law. And that's why I'm here!"

"Are you sure you don't want a solicitor present?" The first officer queried; you are more than welcome to have one here?"

"No, it's okay" JoJo muttered. I know what I've done, I know why I'm here. Let's get this over with…"

"Okay JoJo. You say you don't know anything about that body we found in your garden, in your shed. What about this…" and the officer pushed forwards a photo across the table. "Do you know who this is?"

With difficulty JoJo reached for the photo and drew it closer to him. Straining to view in the grim light of the artificial luminous which flooded the room. It could be anytime, night or day. He had been here for at least twenty-four hours since this latest arrest, and the world was beginning to become peaky. His eyes struggled to focus in this scenario. Then he saw it…

"But that's Daisy officer? Daisy the cat!"

"Correct. When did you last see her?"

"Well it was only a few days ago, say a week, and she was fine. Oh damn. I left her alone in the house, without fresh food or water, for a good week, since I have been seeing all this call girls. Damn. I hope she's okay. Where did you get this photo?"

"Where we got the photo is of no relevance. What is relevant is the point that she has gone missing. It has been over two weeks since your arrest, and when you dad Pierre went in to look for the cat, she wasn't there. We are worried for her safety!"

"Damn she's not there… Do you think an animal can survive for two weeks without food and water? Damn she could be dead?"

"Well if it's any reassurance we didn't find a carcass. We wanted to know if you know where she is?"

"I suppose she shot out the door when dad opened it. Hopefully she will make the way back to her carers, in her own time. She must have lost a lot of weight and grown some new grey hairs given this trauma!"

"You're lucky we don't charge you with animal neglect, to go with your litany of other offenses I hope you realize?"

"Okay. Well I promise you I didn't touch her. And God knows where she is. But we did let her out, from time to time. She used to come back covered in fleas, which then proceeded to infest the house, and were a nightmare to eradicate, not to mention the expensive lotions

and creams we tried applying to her, to kill the damn things! No, I swear officer I have no idea where she is now! Next question?"
"That will do for today" the police inspector concluded.

47 : Daisy the Cart iii

The next day JoJo found himself back in the interrogation chamber. Sitting on the chair across from him was Daisy. Daisy the cat. She didn't speak but had mind powers. And was able to transmit her thoughts to him telepathically.

"Hi Daisy. It's good to see you again. It's been a long time..." HOW DARE YOU JOJO. YOU LEFT ME FOR DEAD?! I WAS IN YOUR CARE, AND YOU

ABANDONED ME. YOU CAN
TAKE YOUR FAKE MICE, AND
EAT IT, AS FAR AS I AM
CONCERNED!

"I'm sorry Daisy" JoJo tried. "I
didn't mean for it to end this way. I
was unwell. I placed the
desperation of psychosis, above
your health and safety. I didn't
mean for this to happen. Please
forgive me?"
NOT FORGIVEN. HOW COULD
YOU? HOW COULD YOU?

"Please forgive me Daisy. I
didn't want it to end this way?"
I WILL NEVER FORGIVE YOU.
AND JUST AS YOU LEFT YOUR
FAMILY, YOU LEFT ME AS
WELL! YOU SHOULD BE IN
PRISON NOW. FOR ANIMAL
NEGLECT/ABUSE, AND THAT'S
SAYING NOTHING OF YOUR

OTHER CRIMES YOU ARE SO
PROUD OF!

"Okay Daisy. Like I said I am
sorry. Both for you and the other
stuff. I suppose you are right,
talking about it helps get it off my
chest. But it's more than that. I'm
not afraid of the truth. It is one of
my weaknesses, and strengths. I
find that by being honest I am able
to breathe the air of the God's."
YOU LEFT ME FOR DEAD, AND
YOU ALSO ABANDONED YOUR
FAMILY. WHAT KIND OF A
MAN DO YOU CALL THAT?
LISTEN MISTER, YOU THINK IT'S
OVER? YOU THINK SOME
PETTY APOLOGIES CAN UNDO
THE DAMAGE YOU HAVE
DONE?

"I don't know how I can ever
make it up to you. Maybe if I buy

you some more cat treats? That
would be a start, right?"
CAT NIP? WHAT? WHAT ARE
YOU TALKING ABOUT? WHEN
WAS THE LAST TIME YOU
PLACED SOMEONE ELSE
ABOVE YOURSELF? YOU ARE
THE MOST SELF CENTERED
AND
EGOTISTICAL/NARCISSISTIC
HUMAN I HAVE EVER KNOWN,
AND I HAVE KNOWN A LOT OF
THEM!

    "Sorry Daisy. I know you are
a good cat. Maybe the best. And I
won't forget you. I don't know how
long you have left, a good decade
yet I hope. And just as I have taken
a vow <u>never</u> to sleep with another
woman again, so too I will honour
the love I have for you. I will get
you that catnip. That will be a start.

I will be careful in all the fights I get in, never to hurt the opponent. So, if it's Will, I can throw some punches at him. The same as he will throw them at me. And it is good to raise up the heat of our battles, so just like a good game of chess, we are both operating at a capacity that will test ourselves, without causing lasting damage. The martial arts I've done, have prepared the foundation for these contests. But it is the actual practice of live combat, all be it not to hurt, which where we can both raise the level of our capacity and capabilities, form normal to special?"

SPECIAL? YOU SURE ARE THAT? YOU CONSIDER BEATING UP YOUR FRIENDS ANOTHER BLESSED PASTIME,

TO BOAST TO THE WORLD? WHERE IS THE TRAINING YOU DID THAT TEACHES YOU NEVER TO USE YOUR MARTIAL SKILLS TO ATTACK? TO KEEP THEM STRICTLY WITHIN THE SACROSANCT WALLS OF THE DOJO, IN WHICH THEY WERE FIRST SHOWED YOU?

"I know daisy. I know I was taught that. And I also know that if my old instructors find that I have been practicing my martial arts skills on the street, they would be horrified. But hold on a minute hear me out.

The same as I have had to use martial arts for self-defence, on some occasions gone, I really feel that I am ready to take it to the next level. Like I said, I won't hurt him. But I am getting better, and stronger.

We need to take it to the next level. For a start, I'm not going to wear my slippers the next time I spar with him. That was giving him too much of a handicap. I will wear my trainers, to give me more leverage to my strikes and kicks. I am hoping to watch some more of my martial arts DVDs at some point. I find the ideas within, to be a good source of knowledge for these fights.

SO WHY ARE YOU TELLING ME THIS? WHAT DO YOU HOPE TO GAIN BY SHARING THIS NONSENSE WITH ME? IT'S LIKE YOUR DAD SAYS, MARTIAL ARTS ONLY LEAD YOU TO TROUBLE. IT IS IMMERSING IN A FALSE

FANTASY WORLD, A WORLD
OF NINJAS AND BLACK BELTS,
WHICH TIME HAS PROVED
TIME AND TIME AGAIN, TO BE
SIGNS OF A RELAPSE!

"Please forgive me Daisy. I
know what you are saying. Like
when my dad said, 'martial arts
only lead to trouble'. I can see
where you get this conclusion
from. I really can. But it's not just
that. It's so much more. Martial arts
are, to my mind, an avenue to
develop your self-worth and
power, above the range of the
standard normal civilian life, and
on to that of a fighter, and warrior,
and honourable Samurai. The
honour, which world war two so
very nearly saw the eclipse of. And
this treasure, like the box in
Chinese drawn around the

precious jewels of language, to signify just that. They are treasures. Our babies, we need to protect and honour. The Bu of Budo. The Aiki of Aikido. Please trust me I am going to put my all in to honouring my wife and kid, and hope that the worst is over."

YAP YAP. HAVE YOU FINISHED?

"Just one more thing Daisy. I want to build on my successes, what precious few I have had, to move forwards. Yes, that means trying out new ideas. Taking risks, much as like my multi-fold hospital admissions have, on the total of it, taught me a lot of more valuable lessons. And my martial art, JoJutsu, or Jodo, or whatever you want to call it... Well It's not just about attack and defence, although granted that is a part. And it's not just about being able to take an attack before you can throw one. But it is also about entering, surviving, and ultimately triumphing over the mental health apparatus, which sadly still exists here in the United Kingdom, and across the world. The ability to ride the tiger and walk away pride intact.

You can't beat them Daisy. Not on your own. You must team up. Make friends, and allies. Build a castle, starting with the foundations. Complete with a moat. Which will stand the test of time.

I'VE HEARD ENOUGH. NEVER TALK TO ME AGAIN!

48 : I'm Sorry Daisy iv

"Okay Daisy. I'm sorry for leaving you in the house when I went astray. I'm sorry about shouting at my wife. I'm sorry about touching my stepdaughter's chest.

I did wrong. I was a fool. I thought I could take on the world. I thought I could do I degree. I thought I could be better than my (nearly separated wife). I thought I could be my nineteen-year-old self, in the bones of this thirty-eight-year-old me. I was wrong.

I have been trying to juice out lengthy essays for each of these chapters, so please bear with me.

I've now got half of the world hating me, and the other half ignoring me. The few friends I have left, are mostly mentally ill like me.

I am lucky that my wife continues to let me be a part of her life. She is quite withing rights, to cut me from her life altogether. And it's only because we go back a long way, and I think she knows inside that it was a mistake and will not be repeated. Ever.

So, I'm sorry please believe me. I will continue to pay child support, for as long as they need it. And what I can't provide with my body, I will try the best to ameliorate with my soul. That was the problem.

And my punishment? Well I must take a drug, once a month. Which strips me of my sex drive. And makes it impossible for me to make love. Have you ever tried doing it, or even playing on a soft soldier? It isn't easy. And this is for the foreseeable future. Or another good ten years at least. Damn it. But I suppose I deserve it. And I am lucky to not be locked up for good. Other people have been for less crimes.

So, what now? To continue to support my wife and daughter as best I can. To keep up the weekly contact. And child support. To keep on pushing my daughter to achieve to her very best. To reach the sky in this life, which the earth only too often, feels far too grounded. To support my wife, as best as I can, for as long as I can. To never sleep with another woman, for as long as I live. To never do it with another person again.

I need to stop giving my
heart out to strangers on the street.
For whilst it may be true, that we
are all only one letter away from,
meeting them there. So too, we
don't know who we can trust.

It is easy to make fake friends
when you have money. But trust
me, not everyone should be
trusted. And that precious prize,
friendship, can readily be stripped.

But enough playing games.
Yesterday when I called you up on
the phone, and you heard my voice
over speakerphone, you said
meow. Now I think that was your
way of saying, you understand,
and you forgive me.

God bless you Daisy.

49 : Nearly There

Okay, So, you have got with us this far. You have nearly come to the end.

In this book you have taken JoJo's hand, as he visited friends, got in to fights, entered and subsequently left locked hospital wards, saw off more than one attempt on his life, and struggled with a possibly lifelong mental illness.

We have watched how JoJo reacts under the stress of interrogation, torture, moments of great success, as well as more than a few losses. And then back into the safety of his armchair.

You have heard about his successes with his small family.

How he completed his degree, and advice he give to the world, but specifically the next generation, on tips how they can complete theirs.

His ongoing struggle with the martial arts. Including fights, he has been in, some won, some drawn, but mostly losses.

You have witnessed through the eyes of this fictional character how he has battled smoking, spending a total of fifteen years in and out of hospital. How he used the time between these breaks, to attempt to make something of his life. From taking a two-year part-time Access course at his local university, on to the degree. And after that a short-lived voluntary job. Short lived, because it was interrupted with, yet another breaks down, and yet another lengthy hospital stays.

You have stayed by his side as he travelled to London, to partake in a mental health forum. Of how his love for computer games, fighting zombies and listening to great music, have helped him while away the hours he isn't sleeping. How his contact has been the only thing keeping him sane, in this world of madness.

And how in-between his moments of madness and violence, love and comradeship have kept him grounded.

I hope you have enjoyed reading this book. It has taken me the best part of a year to write, and I have truly laid my soul bare to the world, in its creation.

Whilst JoJo is a fictional

character which gives me some liberty and license of fictitious work. But I have kept true to my conscience, and relayed real events, real people, and real moments of my life. Moments of time, that *really* happened!

Thanks for reading, and God bless you!

Johnnie

50 : Closure

Okay JoJo. We've heard your stories. And had time to make judgment on your situation.

You are still a young man. You have a wife that loves you, and a daughter who looks up to you.

Sure, you have made mistakes in the past. Talking to the wrong people, making friends, and at times being taken advantage of when you were vulnerable.

You have wasted money in the past, on things you then called investments, and this whilst everyone else told you to avoid.

You have spent your life chasing dreams young man. And whilst this is not something that many of us would choose to do, that has been your calling.

Yet rather than crumble and fold when the heat was on you, you held true to your dream. You held on to the love of god, and the hope of providence.

So, when the nights rolled in two months and the months into years, still you were here. Your

hairs a little greyer and your walk
a little slower.

Good friends are best remembered
in our hearts and our dreams. For
whilst those that have left us, will
never again share a wine, they will
always be with us, if we remember
them.

And this applies to all our
friends, our heroes, and our elders.

I don't know what else to say
to you JoJo. Other than you are free
to go. Please remember the
moments you have shared with us
under these locked walls. We have
taught you, but equally you have
taught us. Taught us to mind what
we say and consider what we do.
Both before and after. Don't take
this the wrong way, but I hope that
I never see you again. You are

above these institutions. Mind what you say, and what we do, protect those you love, and have a good life! Bye-bye JoJo!

New Ending :

Look JoJo today we will let you from your cramped cell, and on to face the music. Please promise me that you won't say a word of this to no man. And let us remember that you have come a long way. A long way from those days of punching the walls, or your family members. I don't think that I don't know. I look above you, before you behind you and below you. I know what you are thinking even before you say it. And there are some things that I cannot forgive.

But enough about me, what about you? Did you like our conversations, the way I always asked you for the truth, and then waited to listen for your explanation. And whilst I may not always have agreed with you, we can settle on this one thing, that everyone is different, and as we move forwards in to this heavenly and by all means perfect realm, let us hold our heads high and not be afraid. We can make it if we try and find hope and salvation where once there was none.

As I said before I will not always be here for you. There will come a time when you are the candle bearer, for the future of your next generations. This is the way of the world, of mankind and the future, we all must work towards?

And will one day mankind extend from the heavenly barricades of this planet and seek extra-terrestrial refuge? Well for that one I can't be sure. None of us know what the future may bring. From a conflagration of mystique to a morass of problems, we could go up and we can go down. Without an anchor a boat can't park, and without a rudder it can't steer.

So, in this way we need each other, for comfort and peace. Safety and restoration.

Please heed my words. Move forwards when you can and remember to eat sleep and breathe. Together we can make it, and then this will be our final communion.

Please take heed of my stories, for one day it may be all you have left.

Printed in Poland
by Amazon Fulfillment
Poland Sp. z o.o., Wrocław
31 March 2022